# Sky High

## Nicola West

# Harlequin Books

TORONTO • NEW YORK • LONDON
AMSTERDAM • PARIS • SYDNEY • HAMBURG
STOCKHOLM • ATHENS • TOKYO • MILAN

Original hardcover edition published in 1985
by Mills & Boon Limited

ISBN 0-373-02760-5

Harlequin Romance first edition April 1986

With thanks to Don Cameron

Printed in U.S.A.

# CHAPTER ONE

'It was certainly a nice hotel, that was one thing.'

Sandie Lewis smiled wryly as she remembered how she had stepped out of the taxi, fair hair blowing round her face and looked thoughtfully at the façade. Perhaps her doubts had been unfounded after all, and the next two days were to be, as Denis had assured her, nothing more than a business conference, with her present to take notes as his secretary.

That was the trouble really—she could never be sure whether she might be misjudging Denis. All her instincts told her to be careful—yet he'd never actually said or done anything to make her feel so wary. It was just the way he looked at her sometimes ... a certain note in his voice as he suggested dinner after a late day at the office, or asked her to accompany him to Guernsey on business. And the way, once or twice, that his hand had trailed lightly down her back as he helped her on with her coat ...

Well, she had thought it all out and made up her mind to come, telling herself that secretaries went away with their bosses every day and it didn't have to mean a thing. And if Denis did have anything in mind, she could handle that, couldn't she? She was twenty-three next month, had been looking after herself ever since she'd first left home at twenty, and she'd fended off enough unwelcome advances by now to consider herself quite an expert at it. One more was not going to make much difference—even if it did come from her boss. And if it made things awkward—so what, a girl with her qualifications could always get a job, even these days.

Denis finished paying the taxi-driver and came round to the pavement. He gave Sandie a quick grin and picked up their cases, and she smiled back as she followed him into the hotel. A lot of girls would think you were off your head, worrying about whether he was going to make a pass, she scolded herself. Most of them would be only too pleased—Denis Brenchley, high-flying accountant and handsome with it, would be quite a catch. Only not for her. Somehow his film-star smile and smooth good looks did not turn her on one bit. There was something about him—something she hadn't been able to put her finger on—that chilled her slightly. Repelled her. She was happy enough working with him—but anything more was definitely out.

The hotel was as pleasant inside as it was out, with a wide staircase leading up from the welcoming foyer. Sandie stood quietly while Denis checked in, noting that although their rooms were separate, the numbers were close together. Another faint prickle of unease touched her skin, but she shrugged it away. This was the twentieth century, wasn't it—nobody took any notice of that kind of thing nowadays.

A porter carried up their bags and Sandie gave a little gasp of pleasure as she saw her room. It was large and pleasant, with a wide window looking down the hill to the harbour of St Peter Port, a sheltered bay of blue water that glittered in the sunshine between the dancing boats. The town lay spread beneath her, a scrambling collection of roofs jostling for space on the little hills. Beyond it she could see the lusher green of the western end of the island, and just below lay the smooth blue glimmer of the hotel swimming-pool.

She turned as Denis came into the room from his

own, and noticed for the first time that the two rooms were connected by adjoining doors. Her brows contracted a little as she glanced, first at Denis, then at the wide double bed, but he smiled and came across to her, standing beside her and laying his arm easily across her shoulders.

'Single rooms are a bit poky, even in a hotel like this,' he said casually. 'I thought you'd enjoy having a bit more space, and a good view. Like it?'

'Mm. It's beautiful. And the island looks fascinating. I shall have to come back one day for a holiday, to explore.'

'Oh, you'll have some time for that too. I don't intend to spend every minute in conference.' Denis glanced at his watch. 'It's almost lunchtime. Why don't you unpack and then meet me in the bar for a drink? We're due at the offices at two-thirty, and I'm afraid it's going to be a heavy afternoon—but we should have time for a look around this evening, before dinner.'

He went back to his own room and Sandie did as he had suggested, a feeling of relief easing her mind. It didn't look as if Denis had anything on his mind but work, after all. She just hoped it would stay that way.

The afternoon, in the Guernsey offices of the accountants they both worked for, went quickly as the conference proceeded and Sandie was kept busy taking notes. Once or twice she glanced up to see the bright Spring sunshine streaming in at the window, and occasionally she caught herself thinking wistfully of walks along the cliffs or swimming in one of the tiny bays, but for the most part her mind was too occupied to wander. She was surprised when Geoffrey Hadwell, the Guernsey partner, took off his glasses and announced that work was over for the day.

'We've done better than I expected,' he remarked. 'Got those off-shore investment trusts nicely sorted out, anyway. We should be able to wind up the whole thing by tomorrow afternoon. What are you doing for dinner, Denis?'

'I thought we'd have it at the hotel,' Denis answered. 'They've a very good menu. Are you joining us?'

'Can't, I'm afraid—got a client coming over from Alderney, staying the night.' Geoffrey Hadwell glanced at Sandie and smiled. 'Must say I'd rather be spending the evening with you! But there it is—I'll see you in the morning, anyway.'

'Can't say *I'm* sorry,' Denis observed as he and Sandie walked out into the bright sunshine. 'I didn't really want old Geoff horning in on our dinner for two! I've been looking forward to it for weeks.'

Sandie smiled noncommittally. Perhaps it would be a good idea to for go any sight-seeing with Denis, she thought, and said, 'D'you mind if I don't come straight back to the hotel? I'd like to do some shopping—these little streets are fascinating, and I want to buy some duty-free perfume. I'll see you at dinner, if that's all right.'

Clearly, it wasn't all right. Denis looked at her, his full lips pushed forward in a pout. 'I was looking forward to showing you around,' he protested. 'Can't your shopping wait till tomorrow? And I'd like to buy you some perfume myself.'

Sandie shook her head, suddenly convinced that she was right to get away from him for a while. 'No, honestly I'd rather go alone. We could sightsee tomorrow, perhaps.' With Geoffrey Hadwell in attendance, she added silently. 'I just want to potter about by myself for a bit. Call it a feminine whim if you like.' That ought to please his male vanity, though she wouldn't normally dream of pandering to such a thing. But she was determined to have her own way over this—Denis was beginning to look much too possessive, and she hadn't liked the way his hand had cupped her elbow as they left the office.

'Oh, all right then,' he said sulkily. 'But I'll expect you back for a drink in the bar, all right? Or—better still—in the suite. Then you can show me what you've bought and let me test that new perfume.' He let her go reluctantly and turned up the narrow road that led to the hotel. 'Don't be too long, will you?'

Thoughtfully, Sandie made her way down to the shops. Her earlier uneasiness had returned and she felt sure that she was going to have trouble with Denis before the night was out. And having adjoining rooms—a suite, he'd called it—wasn't going to make things any easier.

She sighed. It really was time an ordinary, reasonably attractive female secretary could work with a man without having to fend off his sexual advances all the time. She had left one job already because of such unwelcome attentions. She did not really want to leave this one. But unless Denis Brenchley could be made to see that she just wasn't interested in casual sex, she was very much afraid that that was what was going to happen.

The next couple of hours were spent browsing happily amongst the shops of St Peter Port— surprisingly good shops for a small island, she thought, and then remembered the Channel Islands' reputation for being a millionaires' paradise. People came here to live when they found the mainland taxes crippling, didn't they? So of course they'd have money to spend and could afford the best of everything. The shopkeepers of Guernsey would be foolish not to accommodate them.

Sandie bought the perfume she'd wanted, and a thick blue guernsey. She toyed with the idea of a new camera, but ended up with a fine gold chain. Denis would, she knew, say that he would have bought her any of the things she wanted. But Sandie had never had that kind of relationship with anyone and she was not going to start now. Any little luxuries would be ones she bought herself. And there wouldn't be too many of them, she reminded herself, for she was saving up for something very special indeed—something that Denis, with his feet firmly on the gound, could never even guess at.

Much to her relief, Denis had recovered his temper when she arrived back at the hotel and greeted her with a smile, saying that drinks would be ready in his room as soon as she liked to come through. Sandie thanked him and went into her own room, closing the door between them. She would have a shower first, she thought, and not go back until it was nearly dinner-time. Instinct was still warning her against any prolonged *tête-à-tête*, and she would feel safer once they were downstairs in the dining-room.

But to her relief Denis seemed to have forgotten his possessiveness of the afternoon. He did not try to hide his admiration of her pale green silk dress, setting off her slim figure and fall of pale blonde hair and bringing out the green in her eyes, but neither did he give her that 'undressing' look she sometimes caught in the office. He offered her a drink, talked about the island and some of its points of interest, and escorted her down to dinner, attentive and charming—the perfect host, she thought wryly, wondering if she had misjudged him. And she became even more confused as the evening progressed, with Denis sticking firmly to his role of immaculate gentleman and never putting a foot wrong either in word or look.

It was late, and Sandie was feeling relaxed and contented when they finally went back up the stairs. Her fears forgotten, she turned to smile a goodnight at Denis—and then froze as his fingers reached out to take her key and unlocked the door of her room.

'Oh—but I——' she began, with no real idea of what she wanted to say, but Denis, still smiling, pushed her gently through the door and closed it behind them, keeping his hands on her shoulders. Then he turned her towards him and drew her close.

'No——' Sandie began again, her hands pushing against his chest. 'Denis, I don't want——'

'Don't worry about that,' he muttered, his lips full and hot on her face as she twisted her head away, 'I'll soon make you want. Don't struggle, little Sandie—don't be afraid. I know just how to make you want me—that's if you don't already . . .'

'I *don't*!' Feverishly, Sandie squirmed in his arms, desperate now to get away, but a grunt of pleasure told her that her movements, intimate against her will, were only exciting him further. With an effort, she forced herself to be still, standing like a marble statue against him while he ran his lips over her face and neck before possessing her lips; but at this, her control fled. She just could *not* stand there and let those full, moist lips take possession of hers. A thrill of sheer revulsion ran through her and she twisted violently, kicking, pushing, using hands, feet and knees in her frantic efforts to escape. It seemed that she would never be free; Denis' arms tightened cruelly, his hands hard on her body, fingers biting into her soft flesh.

Sandie lost all inhibitions, scratching and clawing at him in a kind of frenzy, her body a whirl of flailing limbs and streaming blonde hair. He wasn't going to let her go, she thought despairingly as Denis held her even

closer, tighter, the sounds in his throat telling her that
this desperate struggle was just the kind of thing he
enjoyed. He was going to win—she hadn't a chance.
She felt him lift her, carry her across to the wide bed—
oh, *why* had she not realised, why had she not insisted
on a proper single room miles away, on another floor,
in another hotel even—and then there was the sensation
of falling as he dropped her on to the soft covers. And a
moment's respite; a moment's freedom as he released her
in order to unfasten his own clothes, his eyes gleaming
in the moonlight that came in through the uncurtained
window as he gloated down at her.

It was a moment only—but that was all Sandie
needed. With a quick movement, she was off the bed
and by the door. And before Denis could do more than
turn, she had the door open and was outside, running
down the stairs, through the foyer and out into the
quiet street.

Where to go from there, she had no idea. But she
dared not pause. Afraid that Denis might follow her,
she ran down into the town, careless of her appearance,
and then along the harbour wall. Only there, where
there were still people strolling under the moon,
enjoying the soft warm air, did she stop and begin to
think.

She could not go back to the hotel, that was
certain. By a stroke of luck, there had been no
receptionist in the foyer as she ran through, but there
would almost certainly be someone there if she went
back. She didn't think her struggle with Denis had
damaged her clothes, but the silk of her dress must
have been badly creased if nothing else, and her hair
felt as though she had been dragged through a hedge
backwards. And anyway, nothing on earth would
induce her to spend the night in that room—not with

Denis next door. That was completely out of the question.

So where *was* she to spend the night? Briefly she toyed with the idea of seeking out Geoffrey Hadwell. She didn't know his address, but it would surely be in the telephone book. If she rang him, wouldn't he come and fetch her, take her back to his home for the night? But a second thought told her that she couldn't do that, either. It would almost certainly mean Denis losing his job, and much though he might deserve it, Sandie couldn't bring herself to cause that. Apart from the humiliation of telling Geoffrey what had happened— and of everyone at work knowing, as they inevitably must.

No—tonight's adventure was one she wanted most definitely to keep to herself. Tomorrow, somehow, she would get back her belongings from the hotel and go back home. Then—well, she would have to decide just what to do later. Just at the moment, the matter or where to spend the night was the most urgent.

In the end, it proved quite easy. Sandie walked along the harbourside, following the bay round to the darkness that lay beyond the town. There she found a seat and curled up on it, thankful for a warm spring night. And although it did get chilly towards morning, the sun rose early and it didn't seem too long before she was able to walk about again, watching the fishing-boats come in, seeing the ferry from the mainland disgorge another crowd of holidaymakers, listening to the gulls as they wheeled endlessly above the quays and pavements.

All the same, it was a very long time before she felt safe enough to go back to the hotel and collect her things. She packed rapidly, afraid all the time that Denis would come in and begin his assault all over again. But he didn't; and with a sigh of relief she hurried downstairs again and got the receptionist to call her a taxi to take her to the airport.

She left Denis to pay the bill. It seemed the least he could do.

'And that's the whole story,' Sandie finished, leaning back in her chair and looking across at her companion with wide, grey-green eyes. 'Dismal, isn't it?'

'Scandalous would be *my* word for it,' he retorted grimly, setting down his empty glass. 'You really mean to say you've let him get away with it, Sandie? You've just come meekly back, handed in your notice, and walked out without even hinting why?'

Sandie shrugged. 'I couldn't, Mike. I feel such a fool about it all. I should have been able to handle the whole thing better than that—I should have realised his good behaviour during dinner was just to lull me into a sense of security. And to have to roam about St Peter Port all night like a vagrant—well, I feel such an idiot, looking back on it!'

Mike Dornley snorted and lifted the wine-bottle to see how much was left. Meticulously, he poured half into Sandie's glass and half into his own. 'Does that apply to any man?' he inquired sardonically. 'Good behaviour being an omen of disaster? Or is it just this skunk, Denis? Honestly, Sandie, I can't imagine what possessed you to go away with him if you knew what he was like.'

'I didn't—not really. I just *felt* it—and you know how most men would have reacted to *that* statement, yourself included!' Her eyes were grey tonight, the green tone dimmed by the red of her shirt. 'And it was my job to go to Guernsey. We have—had—connections there. It was quite an important conference and he needed me as his secretary.'

'Hm. Wonder how he managed the next day, when you'd gone—or how he explained it.' Mike's eyes rested on her thoughtfully. 'Not that that's important now—not to us. What we've got to sort out is what you do next.'

Sandie's eyes misted with tears. Mike had always been a good friend to her, ever since she had got to know him through her cousin Con. There really wasn't any reason at all why he should take an interest in her disasters—but he always did. Just as now he was preparing to help, to think through her problems when really all she had wanted was a listener.

'You don't have to worry, Mike,' she told him quietly. 'You've got enough on your plate, with Jenny pregnant. I'll find another job easily enough. I'm quite well-qualified, you know, and I can operate a word-processor now as well as type. I shan't be out of work for long.'

'Maybe not.' Mike finished his wine. 'But is that what you want to do, Sandie? Go on working in an office? I thought you had ambitions in another direction.'

'Another direction? Oh, you mean the ballooning.' Sandie's face clouded. 'But that's out now, isn't it? Since Con went away—I've no chance of getting my own balloon yet. That's why I want a good job—so that I can save up.'

'Yes, I realise that.' Mike hesitated, then said, 'Look, Sandie, leave it with me for a day or two, will you? Don't do anything without giving me a ring first. I might—just might—know of something you could be interested in. No promises—it might all come to nothing. But—well, like I said, take things easy, all right?'

Sandie stared at him, a bubble of excitement forming

within her. What could he mean—did he know of some
job she could get in ballooning? But such opportunities
were rare, she knew, and she couldn't think of anything
that might be available. Still, Mike, as a balloon
manufacturer himself, with all his connections, might
know of something ... Her eyes came to life as she
looked at him, grey sparkling with green, and her
mouth opened eagerly.

'Now don't get too excited,' Mike warned her. 'As I
said, it might all come to nothing. But I'll be in touch
again in a day or two and let you know for certain. And
now I've got to go.' As he rose and pushed back his
chair, looking round for the bill, Sandie slipped into her
jacket, knowing it was useless to question him. Mike
could play his cards very close to his chest when he
wanted to. Even so, out on the pavement she couldn't
help turning to him once more with eager questions
tumbling from her lips.

'I told you—you'll have to wait.' Mike gave her a
good-humoured kiss. 'And don't let yourself bank on
it—there could be difficulties. All I can say is, I'll do my
best for you. Okay?' He held her by the shoulders for a
moment, gave her a quick grin and added, 'It's good to
see you smiling again, anyway.' And then he was gone,
his tall figure swallowed by the crowd, and Sandie was
alone.

Still bubbling with anticipation, she turned and began
to walk along the crowded pavement. Could Mike
really mean he knew of a job for her in ballooning? If
he did, it would be a dream come true—a dream Sandie
had cherished for the past four years. A dream she had
not ever thought could possibly come true.

She turned away from the crowds into a park and
found a seat under some trees, where she sat gazing
unseeingly at the spring flowers that coloured the grass

with a carpet of mauve and yellow. Ballooning—a job in ballooning! The very thought was enough to send her thoughts winging upwards into the blue sky, wafting silently over the seething streets below and over the quiet countryside. And she knew that if there were even the slightest chance of such a thing, she would grasp it with both hands. It was just what she needed—a life away from the hustle of business offices, away from the rat-race of the city. A life in the open country, in harmony with the environment, using and adding to the beauty of the skies. A life away from men like Denis, who saw women as a combination of note-taking machines and a means of sexual gratification.

A life she had dreamed of ever since Con had first taken her ballooning.

Con had been just sufficiently older than Sandie for her to look on him as a kind of god. He had lived with her family during the school holidays since the age of thirteen when his parents had first sent him home from the Far East to be educated. Since then he had spent both Christmas and the summer in Sandie's home, flying out to join his parents only at Easter, and to Sandie, five years younger, he had rapidly become an idol, to be worshipped and followed without question. She had followed him across moors and up mountains, along cliffs and into lakes. Together, they had set up camp and built huts in the woods; together they had paddled an old canoe on the river and had sailed a dinghy when in the Lake District. Con had never treated Sandie as anything other than an equal, expecting from her the same as he would have expected from another boy, and she had striven never to let herself down in his eyes.

Inevitably, when Con had gone to university, things

had changed. Sandie was then a sensitive fourteen, just beginning to be aware of herself and to feel an unaccustomed embarrassment when Con returned home for his first vacation, tall and somehow different— more sophisticated but not so much that he was unaware of Sandie's changing figure and unable to feel his own awkwardness. There was a constraint between them that lasted through that holiday and into the beginning of the next; then, as suddenly as it had started, it vanished, and they were back to the old easy, happy relationship once more.

It was then that Con began to talk about ballooning. A friend of his had a balloon, he said, or at least his father did, and Con had been invited to spend a weekend with them and try a flight. 'That's if the weather's right,' he added. 'You can only fly a balloon in fairly still conditions. And you can't use the thermals like a glider can—they're a positive danger. So you can usually only fly in the early morning or evening, when there aren't any.'

It was a foreign language to Sandie, but she drank in every word as eagerly as when Con had talked to her about sailing, climbing, orienteering or any of the other pastimes he had taken up. She watched him go off for his weekend, envying him from the bottom of her heart, and woke early to imagine him floating over the countryside beneath a huge coloured ball. If only she could have gone with him! But she knew better than to intrude on his university friendships. That part of his life was something apart, something in which she couldn't share.

Con returned from the weekend more enthusiastic than ever and spent hours describing his flight, until Sandie could hardly bear it. She longed to have a flight herself, but the idea seemed out of the question. Until a year or so later, when Con came home and announced that he was joining a balloon syndicate.

'A syndicate? What on earth's that?' Sandie's father inquired. 'Some kind of Mafia of the air?'

'Not exactly,' Con grinned. 'It's just a group of people who club together to buy a balloon. They're pretty expensive, you know—several thousand pounds before you've got all the tack you need. There are six of us in this one. We all own the balloon and we have a sort of roster of flights, but it's all fairly free and easy because you can't just go off and fly alone—you need a ground crew. So we mostly go together anyway.'

'What if none of the others can go?' Sandie asked. 'Can you still use it?'

'Sure, if you can get yourself some help.' Con gave her a grin. 'Care to volunteer?'

And that was the start of it. Sandie lifted her head, looking up through the trees and remembered that first flight. The rush and hustle of inflating the huge balloon, nothing but a long strip of crumpled nylon to begin with, swelling to a bulge of colour as air was puffed in and then heated from the fearsome-looking burners attached to a basket that looked impossibly small for four people; the gradual lifting of the envelope until it was standing upright, fully inflated, its colours glowing against the pearly sky of the early morning; the scramble to get aboard the basket, standing close together as Con gave the 'hands on—hands off' order to the ground crew which would tell him when perfect equilibrium had been reached. And then that final burst of heat into the towering canopy, the almost imperceptible lift and the sudden realisation that the people on the ground were dropping away, growing smaller, more distant . . . that the balloon was airborne . . .

It had been just like that, she recalled. No impression of lifting, no sensation of height. Just a gradual dropping away, a distancing, and then the knowledge that the balloon was moving gently through the air across open countryside, above trees and fields, over rivers and streams. Because the balloon was moving with the breeze there was no feeling of air movement; in the basket, all was perfectly calm—except for the excited thudding of Sandie's heart.

'It's magic,' she breathed, staring down over the side of the basket to see the chase car setting off below on its treasure hunt through the lanes. Somehow the ground crew had to keep the balloon in sight, estimate where it might be going, and attempt to be on the spot when it landed—not an easy task, Con had told her, but one that could in itself provide a good deal of fun. But Sandie was not concerned with that now—she could think only of the delight of being up here, above the world, floating along in a silence punctuated only by the short bursts that Con was giving on the burner, looking down to see deer moving through the woods, rabbits grazing in the field, and once a kestrel actually hovering *beneath* them. A herd of cows moved slowly through a field, on their way to early milking; a flock of sheep glanced up without curiosity and went on munching. But she noticed that when they drew near a field in which horses stood bunched together in a corner, Con took the balloon higher and caught an air-current that would take them away from the animals; horses, he said, were notoriously nervous and balloon-ists always tried not to frighten them, or indeed any farm animal. Good relations with farmers were essential, since it was often necessary to land in a field, and everything possible was done to ensure that they continued.

They had come down finally in a meadow, to be met by the ground crew who had successfully predicted where they would land and had already asked permission from the farmer's wife to collect the balloon. And not only had she given it, they announced with glee as the balloon was deflated and once again rolled up and packed away in its canvas bag, but she had also invited them all to breakfast. An invitation that had been eagerly accepted, so that within a very short time they were all seated round the big kitchen table, tucking into eggs and bacon and regaling the farmer and his wife with ballooning tales that had them all laughing.

After that, Sandie had joined Con on many more flights. She had become as addicted to the sport as he was himself and had done her twelve statutory flights, made her examination and solo flights, and taken the written examination that would qualify her as a balloon pilot. It had been hard work, but she enjoyed every moment of it. And then, encouraged by Con, she had gone on to take her aerial work permit, so that she could fly balloons commercially.

They had had such plans, she thought wistfully. Plans of setting up a balloon 'stable', of flying at shows, taking part in international contests with commercial sponsors. It had been her dream in particular, but it seemed that it was just a dream, for Con had been offered a job in Africa and had gone, taking his own new balloon with him. And since then, Sandie had had no more than the occasional flight, just enough to keep her licences going, and had had to find herself work as a secretary while she saved for her own balloon.

It was taking her a long time, she thought, getting up from the park seat to make her way home. But now there was a bright spot of hope in her cloudy sky. Just what was it Mike had in mind? Could it really be what she had dreamed of—a job in ballooning? And if so—just what could it be?

She did not have long to wait for an answer. Mike rang her at her tiny flat later that evening, and she knew at once that the news he had to give her was good. There was something else—a note of reservation?—in his voice. But she ignored that and pelted him with questions.

'Hold it, hold it.' She could imagine him at the other end of the line, holding the receiver away from his ear. 'Give me a chance, Sandie. Look, don't say yes right away. Give yourself time to think. It's a job in ballooning, yes—a job flying, commercially. I said, hold it!' She bit her tongue, keeping her questions back almost by force. 'It's a new idea—one of the country's top advertising agencies is setting up its own balloon flight. They'll put on banners for whatever their customers want to advertise and fly the balloons in whatever locations they want. Not just shows, but anytime. It means a certain amount of daytime flying, which needs experienced pilots, okay?'

'Yes, I understand that. But, Mike——'

'The agency's run by an experienced balloonist, so he knows what he's talking about and he's very particular. You'd have to satisfy him that you could handle the job, Sandie, and he might not be easy to work for. But I've told him about you—told him you're ready to start at once if he wants—and he's willing to give you a try. Now, how d'you feel?'

'How do you think I feel?' she answered immediately. 'It's exactly what I've always wanted to do, Mike, you know it is. What Con and I were going to do. Where do I go? Who do I see?'

Over the line, she heard Mike's dry chuckle. 'One of these days, that impetuous nature of yours is going to land you in trouble,' he observed. 'All right, Sandie. You go to an address in the Barbican, London—I'll give it to you in a moment—and you ask to see Mr Sky Darrington. Got that?' He read out the address slowly, while Sandie wrote it down. 'Sky Darrington. He'll see you tomorrow, so long as you ring and make an appointment with his secretary first.' He paused. 'And—good luck, Sandie. Let me know how you get on.'

Sandie promised to do so, and put the receiver down slowly. A cold finger of foreboding had touched her heart as Mike read out the name. Sky Darrington. She had heard it before—and the sound of it now didn't give her any pleasure at all. Why was that? she wondered uneasily. And just what did it presage for her meeting with its owner tomorrow?

Well, if she wanted the job, she would just have to go along and see. And if Sky Darrington was looking for good pilots, she was confident that she could satisfy him on that score. She would just have to, wouldn't she? Tomorrow was going to change her life—she was sure of that.

And as it happened, she was quite right.

# CHAPTER TWO

THE Barbican offices loomed above the river, tall and glittering in the spring sunshine. At the foot was a patch of garden, a drift of daffodils that bowed and curtsied in the finger-nipping wind. Sandie stood for a moment looking up, hands jammed into the pockets of her green tweed jacket, then took a deep breath and went through the plate glass door. She wondered for a moment whether Mike might be playing some elaborate April Fool hoax on her—but he wasn't the type. It would be too cruel. Nevertheless, these plush offices with their thickly-carpeted foyer and the tall green plants that gave an impression of some exotic lido, seemed very far away from the casual, friendly world of ballooning.

The receptionist was looking at her with a bright, enquiring smile painted on her enamelled face. Sandie gave her name, explaining that she had an appointment with Mr Darrington, and the girl nodded and made a quick, businesslike call to his office.

'It's Floor twenty-one,' she said, nodding towards the row of lifts. 'Mr Darrington's secretary will meet you there.' With another bright smile, she turned back to her work and Sandie walked over to the lifts.

She felt unaccountably nervous as she pressed the button for the twenty-first floor. Or maybe it wasn't so unaccountable after all. She'd done a little homework on Sky Darrington since Mike had told her there was a chance of a job with him, and she hadn't much liked what she'd heard. Oh, he was an expert balloonist—had done several major trips, including one across the Pyrenees and one across Greenland. He was well-known in ballooning circles and if Sandie hadn't met him before it was because while she had been ballooning with Con, Sky Darrington had been out of the country, working in America. No doubt that was where he had gained all his expertise in advertising, though he'd still given plenty of time to ballooning, making several long flights there too.

It sounded ideal. But, talking with Mike, Sandie had sensed that Sky Darrington would not be an easy man to work for. He had fought hard to get to the top, Mike had told her, and he did not suffer fools gladly. 'Not that you're a fool,' he'd added hastily, 'but don't take any liberties with him, Sandie. Treat it seriously, all right?'

'Would I do anything else?' she had demanded indignantly, and heard Mike chuckle.

'Quite possibly,' he told her drily. 'You've never quite lost that flippancy you're famous for. It may well be that Sky will appreciate it—I wouldn't know. But keep it for later, okay?'

Sandie had rung off a few minutes later, still feeling slightly ruffled. Did Mike really think she didn't know how to behave at an interview? But she had an uneasy feeling that it was not just her flippancy that he'd been warning her about. There had been something else—something he hadn't put into words. Something he had left her to find out for herself.

As the lift whisked her up to the twenty-first floor, Sandie felt her heart sink. This interview wasn't going to go well, she was sure of it. And if it hadn't been for Sky Darrington's secretary, waiting as the doors opened, she would have pressed the ground-floor button and gone straight down again.

The girl waiting for her gave her a startled look as she emerged, and Sandie gave an involuntary glance down at herself to see that her dress was all right. Nothing seemed to be out of place—tweed blouson jacket, with matching skirt, topping a soft cowl-necked sweater in a rust that lent a glow to her fair skin and lit up the green in her eyes. Nothing wrong there. She looked up, but the momentary surprise had vanished from the secretary's face and she was now smiling a professional welcome. Probably expected me to turn up in some kind of flying kit, Sandie thought with inward amusement—padded jacket, helmet, the lot. She introduced herself and followed the slightly plump figure through a swing door.

The office interior was even plushier than the approach, she noticed with a faint distaste. Presumably advertisers'—and therefore consumers'—money was being spent on this glittering palace of chrome plating and high-tech furnishing. Desks stood spaced about the carpeted room and the air was filled with the muted chatter of the computers on which girls were doing word- and data-processing. Tall palms echoed the exotic effect she'd seen downstairs, and the walls were lined with wood. From the windows there was a breathtaking view across London, but she was given no time to stare at it, for Sky Darrington's secretary was leading her across what seemed to be an acre of thick mushroom-coloured carpet to the inner office.

'Sandie Lewis,' she announced, and then stood back quickly for Sandie to pass her. There was an odd expression on her face, an expression Sandie couldn't quite interpret—was it amusement or a semi-hysterical terror?—and then she was in the room, the door closing softly behind her, and the man behind the big mahogany desk was rising to his feet, a look of sheer stupefaction on his craggy features.

'*You?*' he breathed, staring at her as if she had suddenly sprouted wings and a tail. '*You're* Sandie Lewis?'

'So far as I'm aware,' she answered, wondering why on earth he should be so astounded. 'At least, I was when I left the foyer.' A quick spasm of anger crossed the grim brow, and she remembered Mike's warning about being flippant. Well, she hadn't even had to say a word to get that look on Sky Darrington's face, so it looked as if that warning had been justified. She'd probably finished any chance she might have had of joining the balloon team with that retort.

Sky was still on his feet, glowering at her, and she had enough detachment to take in an appearance that could have done well in films. Tall, well-built body— not an ounce of fat anywhere, if she was any judge— muscles apparent even under the blue shirt that he wore, his jacket being discarded and thrown carelessly over a chair. Corn-gold hair with a hint of red, waving back from a high, broad forehead and the sort of face that could never be called classically handsome but would be able to make any woman's heart race a little. Or a lot, she thought, catching the quizzical look from the searing blue eyes that told her he knew exactly what was going on in her mind. She felt her cheeks colour and glanced round quickly, wondering whether to sit down in the armchair before the desk, or whether she should wait to be invited. She would have to sit without an invitation if he didn't say something soon—her knees had unaccountably turned weak and a strange shaking was beginning somewhere in her stomach.

'I *am* Sandie Lewis,' she repeated patiently. 'You were expecting me, weren't you?'

Sky Darrington seemed to have recovered himself a little. He sank back into his own chair, still staring at her, and shook his head a little. 'I was expecting Sandie Lewis, yes,' he admitted at last. 'I can't say I was expecting *you*.' He didn't give her time to query this astonishing statement before adding impatiently, 'Sit down, for God's sake. I suppose we'd better go through the motions, if nothing else.'

'Go through the motions?' Sandie echoed slowly as she perched on the edge of the comfortable armchair. 'I don't understand.'

'Don't you?' He'd completely recovered now, she thought, his face a mask, his eyes hostile. 'I think you do, Sandie Lewis—*Miss* Sandie Lewis. What *I* can't understand is just why you've come here at all—how you had the nerve?'

Sandie felt her mouth gape in sheer astonishment; then anger took over and she was on her feet, body shaking with rage as she spat her words at the man seated before her.

'Why I've come here? How I had the nerve? I'm sorry, Mr Darrington, you're just not making any sense. You say you were expecting Sandie Lewis, but not me—well, I *am* Sandie Lewis, and I'm only sorry I didn't bring my birth certificate to prove it! Not that you'd have accepted that, probably, you're so darned cynical. You'll just have to take my word for it, I'm afraid. But as for asking why I've come here—well, I was under the impression I had an appointment for an interview with you, an interview for a job. It seemed quite a normal kind of appointment, but maybe I was wrong about that. Maybe there's some reason why people have to have a lot of nerve to keep appointments with you. I wouldn't know—and I'm not really interested.' She turned towards the door, back stiff with anger, then glanced back. 'I'm sure you'll agree with me that there really isn't any point in carrying this farce any further.'

The deep blue eyes were hooded now, but as she turned back to the door she heard a quick movement behind her—no scraping of the chair on that carpeted floor, no footsteps, more a rush of air as a big body moved rapidly through it. She reached out for the handle but even as she touched it a large, warm hand covered hers and prevented her from turning it. With a tiny gasp, she looked up into the chiselled face and drew back.

'*I* decide when an interview's at an end,' Sky Darrington told her implacably. 'Sit down, Sandie Lewis. Let's start again.'

It would be useless, a waste of time, she knew, but Sandie turned and went back to the chair, seething inwardly but somehow unable to do what she really wanted to do and storm out of Sky Darrington's office and life for ever. The man certainly had magnetism, she thought, scowling as she watched him cross behind the desk and take his own seat again. Their eyes met across the polished mahogany, shadowed green striking sparks off brilliant blue, and Sandie lifted her chin a little. Magnetism he might have, power even, but he didn't have to intimidate her; she was never likely to become one of his employees!

'Now then.' The eyes were hooded again, looking down at a sheet of paper on his desk. 'Mike Dornley's been in touch with me about you. He tells me you'd like a job as a balloon pilot.'

'I would, yes,' Sandie acknowledged, though without much hope. 'But they're not easy to come by.'

'You don't have your own balloon?'

'No, I used to go with my cousin Con.'

'Con Lewis?' Interest flickered in the sharp eyes. 'I've met him once or twice. He's in the Far East now, isn't he?'

'Africa. He took his balloon with him—we were going to go in for it together. Shows, advertising—that kind of thing. It all fell through when he got the job abroad.'

'Hardly a living in it for two of you,' Con commented, and Sandie shrugged.

'I don't suppose we'd ever have done it full-time. But Con had the kind of job that he could take leave from whenever he wanted it, and I was doing well as a secretary——'

'Is that what you've been doing? Why have you decided to leave it?' The question was rapped out and Sandie found herself resenting it as much as she resented the tone.

'I think that's my business,' she flashed back. 'Let's say I just wanted a change.' Not for anything in the world would she have told this arrogant man about the humiliating scene with Denis on Guernsey, her hasty flight back and the notice given in as soon as she returned. 'I've always wanted a chance to do more ballooning,' she muttered, 'and when Mike told me about you it seemed a heaven-sent opportunity.'

'So that's all it is to you. A chance to do more ballooning—at someone else's expense.' Sky Darrington leaned forward. 'This isn't a game, Miss Lewis. I'm not offering the chance to make a few flights as and when you feel like it. This is *work*—turning up day after day at shows all over the country, making flights during the day when an inexperienced pilot could easily come to grief with thermals or windy conditions. This isn't sporting ballooning, taking off if you feel like it, playing a few games like Hare and Hounds. It's going to be damned hard work—and I'm looking for tough, experienced pilots, not young kids with their heads literally in the clouds.' He shuffled together some of the papers on his desk. 'Do I make myself clear?'

'Perfectly clear, Mr Darrington,' Sandie said through tight lips. She knew now exactly why Mike's voice had held a note of reservation when she'd spoken to him, and she made up her mind to tell him exactly what she thought of him once she got out of here. 'You took one look at me and decided I couldn't do it. Well, I can understand that, knowing the kind of man you are. I can——'

'The kind of man I am?' he interrupted, his voice satin-smooth as his eyes caught and held hers. 'And just what kind of man is that, Sandie Lewis? I'd be most interested to know.'

Sandie drew a deep breath. Mike had warned her about flippancy—he hadn't told her to keep her quick temper in check. Not that she would have taken any notice if he had—she obviously had nothing at all to lose.

'You're what's commonly known as a male chauvinist pig,' she told Sky Darrington in a clear voice. 'Male—we'll take that for granted. Chauvinist—well, I've never been quite sure what that's supposed to mean, my dictionary says something about patriotism. But pig *definitely*—except that it's something of an insult to pigs. My own definition would be arrogant, browbeating, conceited and egotistical. You think you can make snap judgements of people and be absolutely right, every time. You think you can look at me and say I'd be no good at this job you're offering, without even beginning to find out my qualifications or asking one single question about my experience. You think you know it all—and I suppose you must know quite a lot about advertising, or you wouldn't be here in this office. But that doesn't mean you know *everything*, Sky

Darrington. Especially about people. And more especially, about women.' She paused and looked at his still figure, green eyes narrowing. 'In fact, I'd say you were a woman-hater, pure and simple. And that's why you were so surprised to see me—yes, and your secretary too, now I come to think about it. You were expecting a man—and the moment you saw me, the barriers went up.'

She panted into silence, hands gripping the back of the chair, her whole body tense. Well, that was the end of any chance of a job now, if she had ever had one. The way Sky Darrington was looking, it was clear nobody had stood up to him in a very long time. He wasn't used to it—and he wasn't going to like it.

'I'll go now,' she said stiffly, turning away. 'You won't want me to waste any more of your valuable time.'

He let her get as far as the door before he stopped her. But he didn't move from his chair this time; his voice was enough. The quality of it, cold and incisive, struck right through to her, and although she longed to disobey it she found herself turning back at his command.

'Wait. Come back here.' He watched from heavy-lidded eyes as Sandie walked slowly back across the pale carpet to the chair. 'Sit down.' He leaned forward. 'So you think I'm arrogant and conceited. And—what else was it? Egotistical and a woman-hater to boot. Well, you may very well be right. But aren't you making one or two snap judgments yourself?'

Sandie bit her lip, feeling the colour sweep into her face. Sky Darrington was just the sort of man who could always put you in the wrong, always have the last word. She stared mutinously at the polished surface of the desk, remaining obstinately silent.

'So let's start *again*, shall we?' He drew the sheet of paper towards him again. 'Just as a formality, of course. I can see that you'll continue to feel aggrieved if you don't get a proper interview, and I wouldn't want that.'

The sarcasm in his voice stung Sandie, but she still kept silent. He was trying to goad her, she knew that. He'd seen that she had a quick temper and he wanted to provoke her into saying something unforgiveable, something, that would justify him in turning her out without going any further. As yet, she reflected bitterly, every word she'd said had been true and he knew it!

He ran his eye down the sheet of paper and Sandie let her own gaze wander around the room. So far, the man opposite her had commanded her attention to the exclusion of all else. Now, for the first time, she was able to take note of her surroundings, reluctantly appreciating the stark simplicity of the office, in direct contrast with the opulence outside. The carpet in here was a dark brown, the furnishings in toning shades to create an effect that was wholly masculine. Two parlour palms lightened what could have been a sombre atmosphere, and there were some good pictures on the walls. But the most arresting sight was the window— an entire wall of glass, giving on to a balcony from which one could surely see over most of London. Even from this chair she could see the dome of St Paul's and the silver winding ribbon of the Thames, and it said a great deal for the personality of Sky Darrington that Sandie could have been in the room for so long without having noticed the spectacular view.

'Right,' he said abruptly, looking up with a disconcertingly bright flash of blue eyes. 'Let's go through it from the beginning. How long have you been ballooning?'

'I started five years ago,' Sandie told him, keeping her voice steady. 'I went as often as I could with my cousin Con, and then when we began to talk about having our own balloon I started to learn in earnest. I did my two instructor-accompanied flights with Mike Dornley and I got my licence just over three years ago.'

'Three years,' he mused. 'That's not very long. What about your aerial work permit?'

'I got it a year later. Con and I did a lot of flying in that time and we were able to get some commerical flights as well. I've flown whenever I could since, and I've also got night-flying rating.'

Sky's eyebrows rose. 'You have? Why did you do that?'

Sandie shrugged. 'I just wanted to get all the qualifications I could,' she said simply. 'I did a night-flight, loved it and wanted to do more. I was thinking of going in for instructor's rating before Con went away.'

'All right, so you're keen.' Sky's tone seemed to dismiss keenness as a kind of childish enthusiasm. 'Are you keen enough to trek around the country to shows, spending most of the day waiting for favourable conditions, flying whether you feel like it or not, often from inadequate and exposed sites, living in a caravan and being totally responsible for the balloon at all times? I don't have to tell you that the pilot's in charge and carries the can for whatever may go wrong. And I hope I don't have to tell you that landing a balloon on someone else's property, without being able to ask advance permission, can require a great deal of tact.' His eyes flickered over her and she thought ruefully that she couldn't have given him a very good impression of her ability to be tactful in the past quarter of an hour. Perhaps he'd even been testing her—if so, she must have failed miserably.

'I understand all that,' she said in a low voice. 'I know it's not going to be easy. It's just something I've wanted to do for a long time. I suppose you could say I've got ballooning in my blood—I'm hooked on it.'

He flicked that aside. 'All right. Enthusiasm's certainly a necessary part of making a success of the job—but it isn't the whole story. I need a lot more proof than that to satisfy me that you can handle it.' He stared at her, eyes like glacier chips. 'You're right in part of your assessment of me,' he said suddenly. 'I don't think very much of women—neither in general, nor in particular. I don't like the way you're all trying to muscle into a man's world, and I don't like the shrill way you go about getting your own way or complaining when you can't. As far as I can see, women's movements are seldom little more than an excuse to throw aside all morals and principles and degenerate into sluttishness, all in the name of liberty. It all seems pretty shallow and artifical to me. In normal circumstances, I wouldn't dream of employing a woman for this kind of job, but one of the pilots I'd engaged has been badly hurt in a ski-ing accident and won't be flying again for a long time, if ever. I'm having difficulty in filling the vacancy and there are engagements coming up that I have to meet.' The bright stare travelled slowly over Sandie's flushed cheeks. 'And you needn't look so indignant, either,' he drawled maddeningly. 'I'm being perfectly honest with you and in view of your earlier remarks I expect you to appreciate that. Or doesn't equality extend that far?'

Sandie swallowed hard before replying. In fact, she agreed with quite a lot of what he said about women's movements, but she wasn't going to tell him that! Instead, she said, cursing herself for not being able to produce more than a husky whisper: 'Are you saying I've got the job?'

The sardonic grin snapped to a thin line of chiselled lips. 'No, I'm not! I'm merely saying that I haven't turned you down out of hand. There's a lot more I want to know before I take you on, *Miss* Lewis. I want to be absolutely satisfied that you're up-to-date on your knowledge, and on your technique. You'll come back here tomorrow for a written test, and down to my home in the Cotswolds for a practical at the weekend, all right?'

He was not asking her if it was all right, he was telling her! Sandie gasped and exclaimed: 'So you're not taking my qualifications—you want me to take your own examination.'

'That's right. And it'll be a stiffer one than that set by the CAA, I can tell you! I want to be completely certain before I let you take to the air in one of my balloons— and don't complain that you're not getting time to mug it all up—if you're as good as you like to think, you won't need time, you'll have it all at your fingertips. Which is where it needs to be once you're up in that basket.'

'And if I can't manage tomorrow or the weekend?' Sandie demanded.

'Then we forget it. There'll be someone else come along, and I can always fly the balloon myself if necessary.' Sky stood up and began to shuffle papers again. The interview was clearly over. 'Ten tomorrow morning, here, and be prepared to stay all day.' He glinted a look down at her. 'Look on it as one giant step for womankind,' he advised her. 'I'm going against all my principles in letting you have this chance, Sandie Lewis. By the way, what's the Sandie short for, or is it a nickname?'

'Alexandra,' she answered automatically, and he nodded.

'A beautiful name. You ought to try using it occasionally. It would save a lot of confusion.' He saw her to the door. 'My secretary will see you down. Don't forget—ten o'clock tomorrow morning. That's if you still want the job—you may have changed your mind, of course, now that you know what an arrogant male chauvinist pig you'd be working for!'

Sandie stared at him. For a moment, she was wildly tempted to tell him that she'd done just that, that he could keep his job and offer it to the next macho male who came along, and good luck to them both. But the words stayed on her tongue. She might never get such a chance again. If she passed his rotten exam—as she was determined to do—and made a successful flight at the weekend, wouldn't that be one in the eye for Mr Sky Darrington, with all his talk of principles and women keeping their place? And once she had the job—that is if he didn't find some other way to avoid giving it to her—she really need not see much of him. He wouldn't want to travel around the country behind her, keeping an eye on her, even if he did hope to catch her out. People like Sky Darrington didn't spend too long away from their desks—they could not afford to.

'I'll be here,' she said through tight lips. 'Ten o'clock. And I'll keep the weekend free as well.'

'That's fine,' he said pleasantly. 'Until we meet again, then. And you never know—we may both be in for a pleasant surprise.'

For the first time, the mask dropped a little and a look that was all man came into his eyes as he assessed her, taking in her oval face with its frame of soft, pale hair, her grey-green eyes and her slender figure. Sandie stepped back involuntarily, catching her breath as a strange tingling shivered through her body and down her spine. Oh no, she thought in disgust, you're not catching me *that* way, Sky Darrington! That's just what I came here to avoid. And if that's going to be your approach, you won't see me for dust, balloon or no balloon. Dalliance with the boss was out—but definitely out.

She determined that any future encounters with Sky Darrington must be conducted on severely formal lines. Even if he did give her that oddly exciting, unfamiliar tingling at the base of her spine.

Or maybe because of it.

# CHAPTER THREE

IT was almost seven in the evening when Sandie's train drew in at the station at Moreton-in-the-Marsh on the following Friday, and she collected her luggage and got out on to the platform, looking about her warily.

She hadn't really expected to be here at all this weekend. The written examination, which had taken all day to complete, had been every bit as stiff as Sky had promised, and Sandie had left the offices feeling drained, convinced that he would not pass her. He hadn't even told her what pass-mark he was setting, which she considered grossly unfair—but he was the piper and could call the tune for this particular dance. There was nothing at all that she could do about it.

It had been a surprise, then, when Sky had telephoned her a couple of evenings later and told her that he would be expecting her for the weekend. Sandie had held on to her tongue, asking only if he had seen her papers, to which he'd given a brief 'yes'. No indication as to whether he had actually examined them—but surely he must have, or he wouldn't be wasting his time with her this weekend. And he certainly wouldn't be inviting her to his home. She wondered suddenly if he had done this with all the other pilots he had interviewed, and guessed that the answer was probably no. They, presumably, had all been men. . . .

Sandie turned as quick, firm footsteps on the platform told her that Sky Darrington was approaching. He seemed even bigger here, she thought, looking up at him, seeing the brightness of his hair against the dusky evening sky. He probably saw her as nothing but a scrap of flesh and bone—hardly big enough to handle a Christmas balloon, let alone a full-sized, hot-air one. Perhaps if she had been a big-boned Amazon, his attitude might have been different—though she doubted that, knowing his attitude to women in general.

'Well, you wanted a woman-hater, didn't you?' Mike had asked when she had phoned him to expostulate over his sending her to Sky without revealing that she was a woman. 'I knew he wouldn't see you if he did know—but you've got a chance now, and at least you won't have the trouble with him that you had with Denis!'

I wish I could be as sure, she had thought, remembering that assessing look in his eyes as he'd seen her out of the office. But perhaps she had been mistaken about that—he'd been coolly formal and polite when they had met again the following day, had sat her down in a corner of his office to do her examination and had taken no further notice of her as she sat wrestling with the questions on maps, navigation, airmanship and meteorology. She quite clearly meant no more to him than an extra piece of office furniture, brought in for the day.

His look was just as impersonal now, as he bent to take her suitcase and led the way from the station. Sandie followed meekly, unable to repress a tiny thrill of excitement. Whatever else it might prove to be, this was a weekend away, a weekend in countryside she'd never had a chance to explore before, and there was ballooning in it too. Even if Sky didn't take her on— and she did not think for a moment that he would—she would have had another flight. Maybe more than one. She would not have lost anything.

'It's about twenty minutes to the house,' Sky told her as he swung the gleaming Mercedes out of the station yard. 'Dinner's at eight, so that should give you time to change. Did you have a good train journey?'

Formality was obviously to be the order of the day. Sandie wondered if he would be able to keep it up once they started ballooning. 'Yes, thank you,' she answered politely. 'It was really quite quick, though rather crowded.'

'Yes, I'm afraid that train usually is, especially on a Friday.' He concentrated on his driving as they plunged into narrow lanes bordered by hedges already beginning to show a shimmer of pale green, and conversation lapsed. They both remained silent until they came to the village where Sky lived, driving through the street of picturesque, thatched Cotswold cottages before he swung off through tall wrought-iron gates and along a drive that climbed a gentle slope of green pasture before arriving at a long, low house.

'Oh—it's lovely,' Sandie exclaimed involuntarily, and craned her neck to see better.

Sky gave her a quick look and pulled up so that she could take in the whole of the house. It was no more than two stories high, with tiny dormer windows peeping through the old stone tiles on its roof, and the rich colour of the sunset gleamed gold on the lead-lighted windows, warming the mellow walls to a soft amber glow. Later, there would be roses to paint extra colour on those walls, but now the flowerbeds at their feet were a mosaic of mauve and yellow and white, a patchwork of crocuses with the taller daffodils standing protectively behind. Past the house she could see the gnarled, nursery-rhyme shapes of old apple-trees, while beyond the orchard the rolling Cotswold hills rose to shelter the house from the winds that blew from north and east, keeping it secure and safe from the worst of the winter weather.

'How long have you lived here?' Sandie asked, her determination to stay cool forgotten in her delight.

'About three years. I bought it when I came back from the States. I was brought up in the Cotswolds, though not here, and it's very handy for London. Good for ballooning, too,' he added casually.

'Yes, I should think it is.' Sandie looked about her as the car moved forward once more, imagining the drift of a balloon across those rolling hills. 'Have you heard a weather forecast for the morning? It looks quite settled now.'

'I rang the local RAF station. They think it should stay quiet.' He gave her a sideways look. 'I hope you're not thinking of this weekend as some kind of spree. I warn you, I'm serious about this business—if you fly for me, you've got to be *good*.'

At once, Sandie's rising spirits were deflated. She bit her lip, suppressing the annoyance that he seemed to rouse so easily in her, but couldn't help asking tartly, 'Well, I imagine that applies to all the pilots you engage, doesn't it—or maybe being *men* means they're automatically good.'

Sky's craggy face twitched, whether with anger or amusement she couldn't tell; his voice was cool and remote as he answered, '*Anyone* who works for me has to be good.' And then they were swinging round in front of the house and he was gentling the car to a halt that barely disturbed the fine gravel before leaping out and coming round to open her door.

If only he weren't so devastatingly attractive, she thought, standing by the car while he hefted her suitcase from the boot. Those sapphire eyes, that firm sculpted mouth, the jutting jaw and the harvest-gold hair—they all added up to an appearance that could have had women flocking. And did, for all she knew. Plus a personality that would command attention in any company. He only had to use charm, as she didn't doubt he could, and he would be virtually irresistible. A tiny lash of fear flicked at her nerves, but she shrugged it away. She was safe enough—Sky Darrington had shown no signs so far of using charm on her, and he didn't seem likely to change now. And if he kept on treating her the way he had so far, as if she were some kind of third- or fourth-class citizen, she would find him very resistible indeed.

With a jerk of his bright head, Sky led her through the oak front door and into the house. He walked casually, accustomed to his surroundings, but Sandie followed more slowly, absorbing every detail of the panelled hall, the wide stairs and the big, low-ceilinged rooms above. Eyes wide and grey in the twilight, she found herself in a spacious bedroom, carpeted with the pale green of a cut cucumber, furnished in deeper green, with curtains and bedcover of warm apricot that offset any coldness in the decor. The leaded-light windows were flung wide to admit the last burnished rays of the sun, and the soft scent of spring flowers drifted in from the garden. The view stretched out limitless to the shadowy blue of the Welsh hills, while nearer at hand she could see the clustered roofs of the village down below, with the yellow tower of the little church rising like a symbol of strength from their midst.

Sky had put down her case and was watching her. Sandie tore herself away from the window, promising herself a longer look tomorrow sometime, and glanced around the room, surprised by the quiet taste shown by the decorations. The bed was wide and looked comfortable, there was a cosy armchair and a round table as well as the more usual fitted bedroom furniture, and on the wide windowsill a huge copper jug filled with daffodils. The whole effect was warm and welcoming—exactly the opposite of what she had expected from Sky Darrington, who had so far shown no warmth or welcome towards her whatsoever.

'Well?' he asked, and she wondered if she imagined that defensive note in his voice. What did *he* have to be defensive about?

'It's lovely,' she said simply. 'Thank you for taking so much trouble.

He brushed that aside. 'Oh, it's no trouble to me. My housekeeper, Mrs Collins, saw to all that. I just told her I had a guest coming for the weekend—a ballooning guest. She knows what that means!'

Sandie smiled. 'Early mornings and late dinners,' she suggested, and he nodded.

'There's no punctuality where ballooning's concerned! Now, if you'd like to change—no need for anything formal—I'll see you in about twenty minutes. There's only us for dinner, but we'd better give Mrs Collins the satisfaction of arriving on time for one meal, at least. You can find your own way down, can't you? First door on the left at the foot of the stairs. Oh—and that door leads to your bathroom. Let me know if there's anything you need.'

He vanished, leaving Sandie alone. Biting her lip ruefully, she crossed to the door he'd casually waved at, and opened it. The bathroom was small but complete, decorated in the same delicate, cucumber-green that made the bedroom look so fresh and pleasant. There was new soap, shampoo and talcum powder in a range that was too expensive for her to buy, and the towels were thick and fluffy.

She could quite easily have spent the evening here,

Sandie thought wistfully, using those delicious toiletries, having a long, luxurious bath. Instead, she would have to find some way of getting through it with Sky Darrington, who obviously found her both uninteresting and downright boring—while she, all the time they were together, was all too sharply aware of that uncomfortable tingling, a tingling that could flare at any moment into blazing temper. Or into something else . . .

It was five-thirty when the alarm clock shrilled into Sandie's ear next morning, jerking her into awareness of the pale light that was beginning to creep into the room. For a few moments she lay blinking, wondering where she was; then she remembered about Sky and the ballooning, and slid out of bed, her heart already thumping in apprehension.

This was to be the real test—Sky had left her in no doubt about that. The written examination had been just a preliminary—now she was to take charge of one of his own balloons, treating him as nothing more than a passenger, while she got the balloon inflated, into the air and on a safe and—she hoped—uneventful flight. The fact that she had never before seen the countryside over which they were to fly was just part of the test. And the ground crew which he was providing were briefed to behave as ignorant amateurs, doing what she bade them and nothing more.

Well, she could cope with all that, couldn't she? Sandie stood at the window, anxiously assessing the sky. She'd taken amateurs on flights before and never worried—why start to panic now? *Especially* now, with so much at stake. For she was acutely aware that she wanted this job very badly indeed—and not just because it was the job she'd dreamed of. Because to make Sky Darrington admit that she could match up to his exacting standards would be an achievement in itself. A blow, if you liked, for womankind, she thought wryly, and smiled at herself. She'd never actually seen herself as a rampant feminist before, but there was something in Sky's manner that made her want to force him to look at women—all women—in a different way, not just as submissive little homemakers or decorative toys for men to play with when they had nothing better to do. For she was sure that this was the way he saw women; he had never bothered to make any secret of it.

Aware that to be late would be to score her first black mark, Sandie went into the bathroom and quickly washed and brushed her teeth. It was cool in the bedroom and would be cold outside, so she dressed in warm corduroy jeans, vyella shirt and thick pullover, picked up an anorak and gloves, then ran downstairs. Sky was already there in the dining-room, a tray of toast and coffee on the table, and with him were two other men, both about Sandie's age, who gave her friendly grins as they got to their feet to greet her.

'Tim Bright and Andy Prior, your ground crew,' Sky said, introducing them. 'They're both in the team, though they're not qualified pilots yet—got a few hours to put in before they can get their licences. We might be able to give them a flight this morning, if I'm satisfied with your performance.'

Sandie gritted her teeth. Satisfied with her performance indeed! She already held all the licences it was possible to hold, had achieved more hours of flying than she cared to count, and had been on the point of becoming an instructor—what more did he want? She gave him a brief nod and then held out her hand to the other two, giving them her most dazzling smile and saying she was looking forward to working with them. Someone appreciates me at least, she thought with an inward grin, noting their expressions of pleased surprise. It was quite plain that neither of *these* two was a woman-hater!

'We'll be off as soon as you're ready,' Sky said in a clipped voice, and Sandie quickly helped herself to toast and coffee. Nobody ever ate a hearty breakfast before going on an early-morning balloon trip—that would mean getting up at an even more unearthly hour!—but they would demolish whatever Mrs Collins cared to set before them on their return. Which might not be until nine o'clock or later—there was no way of knowing how long a balloon flight might be, for perfect conditions occurred too rarely not to take advantage of them, and the length of the trip then would be determined only by the amount of propane available to keep the envelope heated.

A few minutes later they were all out on the drive, scrambling aboard the large van Sky used for transporting his balloon. The balloon itself, securely fastened into its blue canvas bag, was wedged into the big wicker basket and took up most of the space in the back of the van. Tim and Andy huddled on the floor behind it, while Sandie got into the front seat beside Sky.

This was a familiar world to her—she had lost count of the times she and Con had set forth at similarly early hours, a crowd of them packed into a van or car with the balloon as precious cargo. At first, she had been horrified by the demands of the sport—getting up at five-thirty hadn't been one of her favourite occupations—but she knew that later, when the sun began to warm the ground, dangerous thermals would develop which could carry a balloon high in the sky or drop it with an equal abruptness. There was no way of using them, as a glider did, and a balloon's best place during

thermal conditions was on the ground. Which, together
with the winds that could rise during the daytime, was
one of the things that made show flying more difficult.
Organisers and advertisers naturally wanted the
balloons to fly when the maximum amount of people
were around to see them—and that wasn't likely to be
at six in the morning!

The balloon was to be flown from a level field not far
from the house, Sky told her as they bumped through a
gate and across the grass. There was shelter from a
nearby belt of trees, and they would be able to lift high
enough to cross the nearest hills. After that, it was up to
her.

'And before it too, come to that,' he added. 'You're
in sole charge this morning, don't forget—the rest of us
have never been ballooning before and don't know the
first thing about it. In fact, all I know is that you get
hot air from somewhere, but I don't properly
understand where. Would you like to explain it to me?'

Sandie drew a deep breath, fighting down her
exasperation. Was there *really* any need for Sky to take
pretence to these limits? Feeling very self-conscious, she
explained in detail just how a balloon worked—how air
was pumped into the envelope sixty or eighty feet long,
to inflate it, and how that air was then heated so that it
rose, taking the balloon and its basket with it. How the
height to which the balloon rose could be controlled by
letting it cool slightly and then reheating it, and how by
this means there could be some control over direction,
by gauging the strength and direction of the different
layers of air-currents as the balloon passed through
them and by using them to waft the big nylon sphere
through the air in roughly the direction required. What
direction that might be could never be ascertained until
the balloon was actually in the air, since nobody could

judge just which way the air-currents were flowing or which might be the strongest—it was a matter of taking what was on offer.

The whole thing was very random, she reflected, and this was a greater part of the charm of ballooning. Nothing could be planned in advance—the landing had to be made where and when possible, the ground crew following as if on some mad kind of treasure hunt, one eye on the map and one on the balloon. Sometimes they could predict the landing accurately enough to be there to meet it—at others they would still be feverishly hunting through the lanes an hour or more after the balloon had touched down, catching tantalising glimpses of it above the hedges but never able to find the road that would lead them nearest to it. The situation became even more difficult if the balloonist ran out of propane and had to let the balloon deflate—then there would be no big coloured marker to guide the chasers, and the occupants of the basket would have to roll up the balloon, pack it and carry it and the basket to the nearest telephone—if they could find one—to ring the check number that was always arranged in case of such a mishap.

She hoped fervently that nothing of the sort would happen this morning. Anything like that going wrong would finish all her chances, and as the van bumped to a halt and they began to unload the basket on to the dewy grass, she could feel all the familiar excitement stirring her blood. Her apprehension vanished. This was a world she knew and loved, a world in which she was at home. She felt confidence flow through her veins, strengthening her, and as naturally as if she had known them all her life she began to issue the three men with orders.

'Right. The equipment's all here—airmaps, altimeter,

thermometer, matches. We've got a good launching site, sheltered by trees, and if you look at those trees you'll see that the tops are just moving, very very slightly. That means there's enough breeze to take the balloon so that we don't just hover, but not too much to make it unmanageable. And it doesn't look as if there's any increase of wind, so that's OK.' She moved across to the cylinders that contained the propane gas, checking that they were all full. 'Let's get the balloon out then.'

The big canvas bag was rolled on to the grass and unlaced so that the long, brightly-coloured nylon envelope could be stretched out to its full length. It lay there, crumpled like a discarded ribbon, while Sandie enlisted the help of Tim and Andy to drag out the basket and get it upright while she rigged the frame, feeding the lines from the balloon through her fingers to attach them to the basket, then connected the fuel system, and tested the burner.

Now came the moment of inflation. Vibrantly aware of Sky's critical presence, Sandie tipped the basket over, directing the burners towards the mouth of the envelope. Andy held it wide while Tim blew air in from the petrol-driven fan, and the nylon began to billow out, a great coloured bulge that grew rapidly until the balloon was almost fully inflated. By now, Sandie had directed Sky to the crown, where he performed the tug-of-war that the balloon always wins, leaning back on the long rope and walking in slowly as the top of the great sphere rose inexorably into the air. Carefully, gauging the time of the bursts, Sandie sent great flames of heat into the balloon from the burner. The balloon was full now, rising to stand almost upright over her head. She could feel the gentle, insistent tug that told her it had become, to her at any rate, a living being, a viable creature that wanted to be off, away from the shackles of earth and into its proper element of sky and air and space. The familiar excitement and longing gripped her too; with a quick movement, she tipped the basket back into its upright position and jumped in.

'All aboard who's coming aboard,' she sang out gaily, and Sky ran back from the crown and scrambled into the basket beside her. Sandie gave him a startled glance; she had forgotten for the moment that this flight was in the nature of a test of her abilities, and the knowledge brought with it a sense of deflation, as if she had let the heat die out of the great canopy above her and the whole mass of nylon had collapsed about their heads. But there was no time for introspection. Tim and Andy were beside the basket, hands on the suede-covered rim, and she had to concentrate on the take-off, giving them the 'hands-on, hands-off' orders until she could feel that the balloon was in perfect balance; and then, with the last 'hands-off' order, letting the balloon lift gently into the air, watching Tim and Andy grow smaller beneath her as they turned to make for the van, experiencing once again the delicious peace and magic of her first, and every, balloon flight.

Once in the air, floating above the trees and climbing steadily, she was able to glance at her watch. The whole exercise, from arriving on the site, had taken just twenty minutes—reasonably good considering that she had never seen the balloon before and was working with a crew who were supposed to be inexperienced. In fact, she was gratefully aware that although Tim and Andy had waited for her orders, they had lost no time in carrying them out and even Sky had not, as she had half-expected, made the task more difficult by pretending to make mistakes. The launch, she told herself with relief, had been entirely smooth and successful—a good start to her test.

They were drifting over the Cotswold uplands now, swooping across wide, gently undulating fields that rode high above the cosy villages of the valleys. Sandie could see a long ridgeway, now a modern road but once, surely, an ancient track used by drovers and salt-bearers. The Romans had lived here, she remembered, and many of these long straight roads were part of the heritage they had left. There were villas and settlements too; the Roman remains at Bath and Cirencester were world-famous and attracted many visitors each year.

Concentrating on keeping the balloon heated and at a good height, Sandie studied the terrain. You had to be watching out for landing-places almost as soon as you had taken off, just in case of a sudden change in conditions. There were other things to watch for, too—cows or horses that might be frightened by the sudden whoosh of the burner above their heads, or even by the shadow of the balloon passing over them. Power lines could be a hazard, but these were generally marked on the Ordnance Survey map, and certain areas were out of bounds because they were approach paths to airfields. There were also regulations about height, different according to whether you were flying over town or country. Out here there was no reason why she should not fly as low as she liked, and Sandie took the balloon down to treetop level, leaning out over the side of the basket to pick a few leaves before sending the balloon up again with another few gusts from the burner.

'Very clever,' Sky commented ironically. 'Every beginner's joy.'

Sandie bit her lip, feeling the colour swarm into her cheeks. So he hadn't forgotten his antagonism, even up here where everything was so peaceful. She glanced up at him, suddenly acutely aware of his nearness in the confined space of the basket. There was room for four, standing very close together—but even with two it suddenly felt crowded. Above them, the envelope swelled out like the dome of a cathedral, the early morning sun shining through the coloured panels to make them glow like stained glass. Somewhere below, the chase car was following, waiting in lay-bys perhaps to see which direction they would take before setting off again through the twisting lanes. But between the two— balloon and chasers—she and Sky were alone, suspended in the air, as alone as if the world had ceased to exist. And Sandie felt very vulnerable; and very aware of him.

Sky moved a little nearer, setting one hand on her arm and drawing her into the centre of the basket so as not to upset the equilibrium. Not the balloon's equilibrium, anyway, she thought as the blood began to surge through her brain—she wasn't making any promises about her own. That vital magnetism of his was surrounding her, pressing on her, making it difficult for her to breathe though the blood was pounding in her ears. She stared up at him, unable to tear her gaze away from the searing blue of his eyes, unaware that her own were wide and green like depthless forest pools, unaware that his own breath had quickened and that the fingers on her arm tightened not from cruelty but from a sudden bite of unexpected feeling.

'Hadn't you better give us a bit more heat?' he murmured, and the spell was broken. Shaken, Sandie wrenched her thoughts back to the balloon. In fact, it needed only a short burst of the flame to keep it on its path, but the tiny episode had thrown her and she fumbled with the burner so that the balloon, after the few moments it took for it to respond, soared a little higher than she had intended. Not that it mattered—but she knew without looking at him that Sky would have noticed her clumsiness, and she knew too that the fact that he had distracted her would be no excuse. The pilot ought not to allow distractions, and the fact that she had done so would be a mark against her.

Her cheeks hot, Sandie stared out over the countryside, concentrating on her flight path and making an almost mechanical note of all the things a pilot should take into account—tall trees, woods, hedges, a wisp of smoke from a farmhouse chimney that told her which way the wind was blowing at that height, a chain of power lines and pylons striding across the hills, a village with church tower and flagstaff nestling in a hollow. She was almost thankful for the knowledge that Sky was watching her more critically than she had ever been watched before, even when taking her official examination. Knowing that every mistake would count against her in her bid to land the job she'd always dreamed of was a wonderful aid to concentration, and concentration was the only thing that would keep her mind—and body—off that disturbing awareness of Sky's presence.

They floated on, looking down at the living map of the Cotswolds spread beneath them. People were beginning to appear now, early workers setting off in cars or waiting at roadsides for transport, farmers herding cows in for milking, the odd jogger loping along the lanes. Most of them had their minds and eyes firmly fixed on their destinations and didn't glance up, but occasionally a car would waver suddenly as its driver caught sight of the gaudily-coloured globe above his head, and one or two drew in by the hedge so that the occupants could get out and stare, some of them waving good-morning. The gamekeeper, patrolling his

woods, saw them but didn't wave; neither did the other
man, whom Sandie guessed to be a poacher, making his
furtive way with loaded bag from the other side of the
same wood. As they passed over a small cluster of
council houses a little boy ran out into the garden,
shouting and waving excitedly, and a moment or two
later children erupted from all the other houses and
Sandie let the balloon descend a little so that she could
call down to them and answer their shrill questions.

As on all flights, she was reluctant to descend but
knew that after almost an hour in the air it was time to
start looking seriously for a landing-place. The chase
car was in view, crawling along a main road, and
Sandie peered down, looking for a field with access to
the road or at least a driveway that would provide an
approach. Nobody liked having to carry the deflated
and packed balloon and basket too far—it was at that
point, Con had once remarked, that you began to
wonder if balloons were really lighter than air!

They were flying over pasture land now, some fields
occupied by cattle, others empty. Sandie began to make
her pre-landing checks, making sure that the rip-line
and valve-line were close at hand, switching to a fresh
fuel cylinder so that she should not run out while in the
critical landing-phase, and seeing that any loose objects
were safely stowed or wedged where they couldn't fall
about and do any damage.

'We'll land in that field there,' she announced,
pointing, and Sky nodded as she opened the vent to
cool the air and instigate a slow, steady descent. Over
the last hedge—a last 'half-way down' burn—then a few
yards' flight only inches above ground before the
touchdown. A slight bump; a rise of a yard or two into
the air, down again and a second bump, a faint lurch
and at the same moment a quick pull on the ripcord, so

that the parachute at the crown of the balloon was pulled out to its fullest extent and the canopy deflated, collapsing in a trail of colour that streamed out behind the basket. Almost in the same movement, Sandie extinguished the pilot burner and burned off the fuel, and suddenly everything was still and silent; there was only the sound of birdsong from some nearby trees and then the shouts of Tim and Andy as they opened the gate and ran across the grass towards the basket.

Sky and Sandie climbed out. Sandie was feeling as deflated as the balloon but she smiled mechanically and answered their remarks, apologising for not having kept the balloon up so they too could have had a flight but saying that she had supposed Sky wanted her to carry out the full procedure from beginning to end. 'Which means I'll have to make you pack it up,' she added with a rueful smile. 'I'll empty the fuel lines and check the valves if you'll roll up the envelope. Did you get permission from the farmer to bring the van in?'

'Yes, and we've been invited to breakfast,' Andy told her. 'But I said no, because we knew Mrs Collins would be expecting us back, so we're just having a pot of tea as we pass the house.'

'Mind, I think we'll be lucky to get away with that,' Tim added with a grin. 'There was a whole heap of bacon going under the grill when I peeped in, and practically an entire home-made loaf being sliced up. Bacon sandwiches is my guess, and very welcome they'll be too, as well as Mrs Collins' breakfast!'

The sandwiches turned out to be toasted, and they were indeed welcome. Relaxed at last—nothing that happened now could make any difference—Sandie felt, for the first time, at home in Sky's company as they sat around the table in the big farmhouse kitchen, eating piping hot toasted sandwiches, drinking mug after mug of steaming tea, and recounting ballooning yarns to the fascinated ears of the farmer and his wife. It was a scene any balloonist would find familiar, she thought, warmed by the food and drink as she looked around the homely room. A scene that was one of the big bonuses in ballooning—yet another friendly, unplanned episode in a sport that couldn't be precisely arranged and must therefore appeal to all those for whom pleasure in the sport itself must come before competitiveness.

It was strange, she thought, that Sky should be so keen a balloonist. For there was nothing more competitive than the world of advertising. Was there a conflict between the two sides of his personality—a war between the side that must compete, must come out on top and the side that was content to drift, letting the winds of the day take charge? Was that what made him so abrasive, so difficult to get along with?

As she wondered, she glanced up, letting her eyes move over his face, taking note of the harsh lines of his jaw and the almost tender curve of his mouth as he smiled at the farmer's wife. His eyes, which to her had been so cold, were now warm with laughter, tiny crinkles appearing at their corners, and as he pushed back a flop of burnished hair with long, tapering fingers he looked almost boyish, though Sandie knew that he must be a good ten years older than herself. She felt a strange tug at her heart, an almost painful twist that she didn't want to analyse—and then, as if he felt her gaze on him, he turned and caught her eye.

Sandie sat frozen, unable to look away. For a moment, the laughter lingered on Sky's face, the warmth of his glance caressing her eyes and mouth so that the tiny twist of her heart expanded to a fierce wrench that was at the same instant both pain and joy. She gasped, forgetting the others present, wanting to

reach out to him across the table, wanting to feel his
fingers entwined with hers—but even as she stirred, his
expression changed. The warmth died away to be
replaced by a bleakness that was like a blow. He turned
his face away, deliberately, and set down his mug, and
Sandie sat back in her chair, feeling suddenly that she
wanted to cry.

'Time we were off,' Sky said brusquely, getting up.
'It's been more than kind of you to feed us like this,
Mrs Jenkins. We'll drop in on you again sometime,
perhaps!'

They all laughed at this old ballooning joke and the
kitchen became a hubbub of scraping chairs, feet on
stone flags, and voices chorusing their thanks. Sandie
came out last from her corner and found a moment's
silence while the others were in the yard, talking to the
farmer, to add her own thanks.

'That's no trouble at all, my dear,' Mrs Jenkins told
her, round face beaming. 'It's been a real pleasure to us,
it has. We've seen Mr Darrington's balloon before, you
know, floating past up there and I've often watched it
and thought how lovely it looked. It's been real nice to
have you here, and he's a fine man.' She paused, shrewd
eyes taking in Sandie's face, and added: 'They're not
always the easiest to live with, the really good men, but
it's worth it, believe you me.'

'Oh, but there's nothing——' Sandie began, but
before she could finish Tim was at her elbow, urging
her to be quick, and she turned away, cheeks ablaze,
and scrambled up into the front seat beside Sky, who
was running the engine, impatient to be off.

Well, it didn't really matter if Mrs Jenkins had got
the wrong impression, did it? Probably they would
never meet again—Sandie could not see Sky inviting her
down here for any more weekends, whether she got the

job or not. But what, she wondered, had made Mrs
Jenkins feel that there was anything between her and
Sky? Simply the fact that they were together? Or—had
she seen that tiny interchange between them at the
breakfast table? And if *she* had misunderstood it, just
what interpretation had Sky put on Sandie's reaction to
his look?

Biting her lip, she kept her eyes fixed firmly out of
the window as the van made its way back to Sky's
house for breakfast. Whatever he had thought, she had
a feeling she didn't want to know. All she wanted to
know now was whether he was prepared to give her the
job—then she could start straightaway on the engagements he already had fixed, away from London, away
from the Cotswolds.

Away from Sky Darrington.

# CHAPTER FOUR

'WELL?' Sky said, turning away from the window.

Sandie looked at him warily. Presumably he had called her here into his study to tell her whether or not she had the job. He'd kept her waiting long enough for his decision—right through their second breakfast, at which they had demolished bacon, eggs, mushrooms, and kidneys as if they had never seen food before in their lives, followed by what must have been a large loaf of toast and marmalade or honey; through the first part of the morning, when they had sat around feeling that pleasant combination of laziness and achievement which comes to anyone who has been up early and accomplished things before most people have even stirred from their beds; and into the farewells as Tim and Andy dragged themselves reluctantly from their chairs and declared that they had to be going home. 'Lawns to mow and all that,' Andy sighed, and it was only then that Sandie discovered that Andy was married and lived with his wife and small baby in a bungalow at the other side of the village. Tim, she found, had a flat in the nearest small town, where he worked in an estate agent's office, and wasn't married yet.

'Or even engaged,' he added with a bright glance. 'But not averse to the idea—especially with the right girl!' He gave her a wink that had her blushing and laughing, and then he was gone, sounding his horn cheekily as he drove with Andy past the breakfast-room window.

Sandie had expected that Sky would give her his answer then, but instead he muttered an excuse and disappeared into his study, leaving her to roam aimlessly about the house, unsure of what to do. She cleared the breakfast table and carried a tray of crockery to the kitchen, where Mrs Collins greeted her with a mixture of thanks and reproach, and stayed there to chat.

'So you're going to fly one of Mr Darrington's balloons?' the older woman said, stacking the dishwasher. 'Tried to get me to go up in one of them, he did, but I said no. Always kept my feet firmly on the ground, I have, and always will. Why, I don't even like those lifts you get in these skyscraper buildings. You wouldn't catch me living in one of those tower blocks, not if it meant going in a lift every time I wanted some fresh air!'

'But ballooning's not like that at all,' Sandie said, smiling. 'You don't get any feeling of being up high—not like you do when you're in a high building, or on a cliff. It's more as if you stay where you are and the ground drops away. Honestly, there's nothing unpleasant about it.'

'That's what they *say*,' Mrs Collins observed darkly, as if all balloonists had entered into some kind of conspiracy to get her into the air. 'I don't see much to enjoy about the earth dropping away, if it comes to that. And what about air-sickness? I starts to feel queasy in grandad's old rocking-chair!'

Sandie laughed. 'You wouldn't in a balloon. There isn't any motion, you see—the basket's absolutely stable, held between the balloon and the earth. And since you're going with the wind, at exactly the same speed, you don't get any feeling of being blown along. Honestly, you ought to try it, Mrs Collins, it's pure magic.'

The housekeeper sniffed. 'I'll stay where I was born,

on God's good earth,' she declared, as if the air were an invention of the devil. 'But if you enjoy it, Miss Lewis, that's well and good. I wouldn't deprive anyone of what they enjoyed. And I hope you'll enjoy working for Mr Darrington, too.'

'I don't know that I'm going to,' Sandie said, gloom returning as she wondered just how much longer Sky was going to keep her waiting. 'Mr Darrington doesn't seem to like women balloonists much—or women anything, as far as I can see. He thinks we all ought to be in our proper place at home, doing the cooking and running the house. Like you,' she added belatedly, hoping that she hadn't offended the housekeeper, but Mrs Collins nodded sagely as she closed the door of the dishwasher and set it going.

'You could be right there, miss. There's still a lot of men think that way, especially men like Mr Darrington who've always had a woman to look after them.' She began to put away the rest of the breakfast things. 'They don't mind women doing those things, or any other things they wouldn't care to do themselves, like typing and such, but when it comes to the *interesting* jobs—well, those they want to keep to themselves.' She put the butter into the fridge and straightened up, not noticing Sandie's expression of surprise.

'Why, Mrs Collins, I believe you're a feminist!' Sandie exclaimed delightedly. 'Does Mr Darrington know? Or—more to the point—does Mr *Collins* know? What would you have liked to do instead of being a housekeeper?'

'Why, nothing,' the older woman answered. 'I like doing things round the house, cooking and so on. But that don't mean *everyone* has to like it. And it don't mean others shouldn't do the things they *do* like. Just like men do. Some like mending their own cars and doing their own decorating, so good luck to them. Others'd rather pay someone else, and nobody sees anything wrong in that. Why should it be any different for women? We're all just people, after all.'

'Quite right,' Sandie applauded. 'And I like flying balloons, so why shouldn't I? I wish you'd talk to Mr Darrington the way you're talking to me.'

'And so I would, if he ever asked me,' the housekeeper answered robustly. 'But he won't, of course—why should he?' She stopped what she was doing and gave Sandie a sharp glance. 'Not that I'm saying a word against him, you understand,' she said firmly. 'Always been very good to me, Mr Darrington has, and I think a lot of him. He's a fine man—make a good steady husband someday, he will, and lucky the young woman will be who finds herself married to him. And there's been plenty who'd like to try, you can take it from me.'

'Yes, I'm sure.' Sandie felt a tingle low in her stomach as she thought of Sky's brilliant eyes, mobile mouth and rich gold hair. 'But he's not interested in marriage, I hear.'

'I wouldn't know whether he was *interested* or not,' Mrs Collins said, tipping a bundle of carrots on to the kitchen table and taking a knife from the drawer. 'Maybe he's waiting for the right girl to come along. Got very definite ideas about things, Mr Darrington has, and I daresay marriage is one of them.'

'Yes, I expect so.' Sandie wondered whether to offer to help the housekeeper with the vegetables but decided that she had probably already outstayed her welcome in the kitchen. With a smile, she murmured something about having a look round the garden, and slipped out through the back door.

Sky's garden was not as big as it had first appeared.

Most of the land surrounding the house was meadow and orchard, cropped by a few sheep who had young lambs with them. Sandie stopped to watch them, entranced as always by the attractive creatures, then wandered through the gate that kept them out of the cultivated part. This had evidently been planned and created some time ago, probably before Sky's occupation, for mature hedges broke the garden into several small areas, each different and each in its own way as attractive as the others. Just now, the buds were beginning to open, showing a shimmer of palest green over the hedges and shrubs, while the bigger trees remained cautiously bare. Spring flowers starred the ground—primroses, violets both white and purple, grape hyacinths and tiny woodland daffodils. A blaze of yellow forsythia lit up one corner like an earthbound sun and a patch of mauve crocuses lay like a scrap of velvet along the edge of a small lawn.

Sandie wandered among the flowers, only half seeing them, her mind still on Sky. When was he going to let her know what he'd decided? Was it really necessary to keep her waiting like this? He *must* have made his decision by now, surely. Was he just tormenting her, keeping her in suspense deliberately simply to enjoy watching her squirm?

It's not that important, she told herself unconvincingly. It's not the only job in the world. OK, it's the only *ballooning* job—but does that really matter? A few weeks ago you'd never dreamed of it, and you were happy enough. So what's changed?

A few weeks ago, she thought, I'd never heard of Sky Darrington and I was happy enough. And now *everything's* changed. If she didn't get the job, she would probably never see Sky again—or only in the distance, at balloon meets perhaps. Never to talk to him. Never to be with him.

And would that really matter? Wasn't it what she wanted—never to see Sky again? Had he done anything, said anything, that gave her the idea he enjoyed being with her, wanted to know her better? Had he done anything to make *her* enjoy being with *him*?

The answers to all those questions ought to be no. A very firm and unequivocable no. But she could not bring herself to voice the word, aloud or in her heart. She didn't want to know why; she had an uncomfortable feeling that she wouldn't like the answer. All she did know was that this job mattered more than anything else had mattered in her entire life.

When Sky opened his study window and called her to come in, her heart leaped like a salmon making for its spawning ground. She felt her palms, suddenly wet with perspiration; and when she turned to hurry into the house, she was shaking all over.

'Well?' Sky said again, and Sandie pulled herself together, trying to stop the shaking, or at least hide it from his too-perceptive sapphire eyes.

'Well what?' she countered. 'You're the one making the decision.'

'And don't you have to make any decision?' he asked coolly. 'Like, whether you want to work for me.'

'Not until I know there's a chance I could.'

'So you would like to,' he said, almost to himself. His eyes moved up and down her body, clad now in slim-fitting white jeans and dark blue roll-necked pullover. 'You would still like to.'

'I'd like a job as a balloon pilot,' she returned coolly. 'Whether it's working for you or anyone else is really beside the point.'

His fine brows rose. 'Is it, indeed? How do you see this job then, Miss Lewis?' Gone was the friendly, first-

name camaraderie of the morning, she noticed ruefully.
'Do you imagine that I am just going to hand over eight
or nine thousand pounds' worth of balloon, together
with trailer and all the fittings, for you to go and play
with as you please? Do you imagine that you'd see no
more of me, except to sign the odd cheque for
maintenance or fuel? Do you really think that?'

'Well—no. But you work in London—you run the
advertising company, you wouldn't be able to come out
to all the shows and things I'd be flying at. Besides,
there are the other pilots—you'd need to spend time
with them as well—you couldn't just concentrate on
me——' She was floundering badly, disconcerted by the
gleam in his eyes. Was he actually *laughing* at her?

'Believe me, Sandie,' he said quietly, and her heart
leaped as he used her first name again, 'if I give you this
job you'll be seeing plenty of me. I may run one of the
top advertising agencies in the country, but I'm not
shackled to my desk and I do know how to delegate.
And I also enjoy ballooning. Yes, no doubt I'll be
pestering the life out of my other pilots too—but I'll
find time to fit you in, never fear. Now——' he picked
up some sheets of paper and stood regarding them with
a slight frown '—as I'm sure you know, you did very
well in the written examination. Better than I expected.
Better, in fact, than any of the others.' He glanced up
quickly, eyes gleaming again as he caught Sandie's
stunned expression. 'As for the flight this morning, well,
you don't need me to tell you that you passed with—
let's say *flying* colours. It's a pity conditions were so
perfect—I'd have liked to see how you cope in wind or
thermals. But I saw enough to know that you can
handle both the balloon and yourself—and that's what
I was really looking for. In commercial flying, a cool
head is all-important. I must admit, when you blazed

out at me in the office the other day I had very serious doubts indeed. But as long as you confine your temper to the ground . . .' He smiled. 'Welcome to the stable, Sandie.'

'You—you mean you're giving me the job?' she whispered, and when he nodded: 'But—just a minute— let's get this clear. You said I did *better than any of the others* in the written exam? Does—does that mean you made *all* the pilots do it? All the applicants?'

'Certainly. And the flight test, too.' He waited, smiling that maddening, devastating smile.

'But you—you let me think that only *I* did that test!' Sandie burst out. 'You let me think it was just because I was a woman—because you didn't expect me to pass anyway and it would be a way of turning me down! You led me on all along the line, Sky Darrington, and all the time you've just been laughing at me!'

'Not laughing *at* you—laughing *with* you,' he began, but she cut in furiously.

'How could you be laughing *with* me when I'm not laughing at all? I think your behaviour is utterly despicable—sly, underhand and downright hypo-hypocritical.' She wished she hadn't embarked on that word, but got it out successfully on the second try. 'I'd bet six balloons to a teabag that you didn't do that with any of the others. You'll have told *them* that the exam applied to everyone. You didn't tell *me* because you hoped it would put me off—and because you wanted me to feel I had to be twice as good as a man to stand a chance. Well, I'm afraid your amusing little scheme has backfired on you, Sky Darrington. You can *keep* your rotten job. I wouldn't fly in one of your balloons now if you paid me a million pounds. And I feel sorry for those who do!'

She whirled towards the door, but Sky was there first,

leaning back against the oak panels, still with that maddening smile curving his lips. Sandie clenched her fists, wanting to strike him but retaining just enough control to restrain herself. Her eyes blazed green fire, her cheeks flew flags of angry colour and her breasts rose and fell under the clinging thin jersey. Sky's glance moved down, lingering on the rounded curves, then up again to her furious face.

'You don't really mean that, you know,' he remarked softly. 'You don't really mean a word of it. You know you're just aching to fly in my balloons. Just as you're aching for this.'

Before she could realise what he was doing, he had moved closer and laid both hands on her arms. A violent tremor shook her body as he drew her near, just as he had in the basket a few hours earlier. But this time he drew her closer, so that the tips of her breasts brushed his body. As Sandie stared up at him, eyes wide as a cat's, he bent his head and laid his lips on hers.

The kiss shook her as if the earth had rocked. At first nothing more than a butterfly brushing of lips, it developed almost immediately into a savage plundering that took no account of her struggles, deepening as Sky sought the sweetness of her mouth, parting her lips with his own and probing with a tongue that was both tender and strong. Sandie felt her pulses thunder as she hung in his arms, hands pushing feebly and ineffectually at his chest, legs too weak to support her so that her body was kept upright only by the pressure of Sky's and the iron firmness of his arms about her. Her senses whirled; eyes closed, she was aware of nothing but this, this kiss that went on and on, that had become the only reality so that the room, the house, the earth itself receded from her consciousness and when Sky finally let her go, his hands on her arms holding her steady, she blinked at her surroundings as if she had never seen them before.

'I thought so,' he said softly, his eyes dark with an expression she couldn't fathom. 'You've been wanting that ever since you first saw me, haven't you?'

His sheer conceit staggered her, and she felt the relief of clean, healthy anger taking over from the sultry arousal of a moment earlier. *'Wanting that?'* she spat, shrugging his hands away from her as she stepped back. 'You flatter yourself, Mr Darrington! It had never even crossed my mind—not at the moment I first saw you, or at any moment since. Why on earth should it? I told you, I thought you were the most insufferable, conceited and arrogant man I've ever met—and there's been no reason to change my opinion. *Kiss* you? I'd as soon kiss a rattlesnake!'

'That's not the impression you just gave me,' he drawled, lounging easily back against the panelled door. 'There was a definite response there, deny it as you might. Yes, I believe we could have quite a—what do they call it these days?—a meaningful relationship together. Or, if you prefer a simpler phrase, a lot of fun. Don't you? Be honest, now!'

'No, I don't, and I've never been anything other than honest. You repel me, Sky Darrington—you and your chauvinistic attitudes and your archaic belief in man being the supreme being. If you imagined I was responding, you must be even more insensitive than I thought—I was trying to get away from you before I was sick!' She paused, trying not to remember the delicious quiver of her spine as he'd held her in his arms, the tenderness and passion of his mouth. 'If I hadn't already made up my mind to refuse any job you might offer me, I certainly would after that—you can *keep* your balloons, Mr Darrington, and I hope they all go off with an almighty bang. And now—if you don't mind—I'd like to go up to my room and pack. I find I can't spend any longer here—I've suddenly remembered an important engagement at home. Or anywhere.'

To her fury, Sky remained quite still, that aggravating smile still crinkling in his eyes. If only he weren't so damned *attractive*. But at least she'd managed to hide her feelings pretty well, she congratulated herself. He must surely have got the message by now—that she found him entirely repulsive. He wouldn't touch her again—she hoped. If he did—well, that response he'd mentioned might be a bit more difficult to hide.

'Tough,' he remarked pleasantly. 'About that urgent appointment, I mean. Because——' he glanced at his watch '—I doubt if you'd be able to get packed in time to catch the next train from Moreton-in-the-Marsh, and anyway that would mean missing lunch which I'd be very reluctant to do, even after our double breakfast. And the next one isn't until half-past four. Still, if you were *very* quick with your packing, you should have plenty of time to walk it. You might even find a pub open along the way where you could get some lunch. One or two do some quite good bar snacks.'

'You mean you won't take me,' Sandie said through her teeth.

'Not for the next train, no. And really, I'd rather you reconsidered and stayed the rest of today and tonight, as we'd arranged. I'm sure your appointment can wait, can't it?' He tilted his head and smiled down at her persuasively. 'Pity to let just one little incident spoil what could be a beautiful friendship,' he murmured. 'And we've got lots to talk about, you know. Your first show, for instance. Because you *are* taking the job . . . aren't you?'

'I—I wasn't aware that you'd actually offered it to

me,' Sandie stammered, and saw a tiny glint of satisfaction in his eye. Oh lord, he was winning again . . . but she *did* want that job, and she knew it was very unlikely there'd be a chance of another. She would only curse herself later if she turned it down now—and surely she could keep her distance from Sky, now she'd been warned.

'I'm offering it now,' he said. 'On trial, at least. You've satisfied me that you can handle a balloon—it remains to be seen whether you can cope with commercial flying on the scale I've got in mind. It won't be just in this country, a summer job—there'll be foreign trips too, all the big ballooning events on the Continent and in America. And some TV work—I'm negotiating a contract now for advertising featuring balloons, like the Martini advert that was done some years ago. Think you can handle all that?'

Sandie stared at him, excitement tingling through her veins. It was even better than she'd dared to hope! He'd never mentioned any of those schemes before—perhaps he'd been saving them just in case she needed persuading. Her eyes were like stars as she began to speak, but he cut her short.

'I see you like the idea. So we'll take it as read, shall we? And you'll stay the rest of the weekend—to do a lot of talking and maybe a bit more ballooning.'

Unable to speak, Sandie nodded. So long as you don't kiss me again, she wanted to say. But perhaps he would take that as read, too. She hoped so. She hadn't yet sorted out her feelings about Sky Darrington—and until she had, she didn't want any more earth-shaking experiences. She might be able to handle a balloon—she wasn't at all sure she could handle Sky.

To her relief, the rest of the weekend passed without

Sky making any more advances to her. They ate lunch together, talking ballooning throughout the meal, and Sandie found herself beginning to relax. Sky could be good company when he chose, she discovered, and he showed an unexpectedly quirky sense of humour which exactly matched her own. Mike had been wrong about her flippancy, she thought with an inward smile. It went down quite well with Sky after all—though she admitted that it might not have done at that first interview, when she'd got off to such a bad start because he had been expecting a man. He seemed to have overcome that prejudice now, however, and also to have forgotten any desire to exert his masculinity over her in other ways. The memory of the kiss made her shiver again—but she quickly pushed it away. The sooner they both forgot they were different sexes the better. In ballooning, Con had told her, there were no 'ladies'—everyone was expected to muck in and be 'one of the chaps'. She'd be one of the chaps to Sky, and then there would be no more problems.

To her delight, Andy and his wife came to dinner that evening, with Tim roaring up the drive in his little sports car a few minutes later. Sandie was surprised that he had no girlfriend with him—Tim didn't look the sort of young man to lack female company—but soon found that to Tim, at least, she was definitely not 'one of the chaps'. He attached himself firmly to her side all evening, making the excuse that as he was going to be a member of her crew he thought they ought to get to know each other, giving her such a cheeky wink as he said it that she laughed out loud. Well, she would be able to handle Tim all right—not that he'd need much handling. There wasn't, she thought as she smiled back at him and touched her glass to his, a serious bone in his body.

'So you made it through the tests,' he observed, leaning back in a deep armchair. 'I hear they were pretty stringent. Mine was bad enough, and I'm not a pilot—yet.'

'But you're going to be, aren't you?'

'Oh yes, Someday. I haven't bothered up to now—been quite happy to hitch rides with other people. Didn't even bother keeping a log book at first. But this new scheme of Sky's is pretty exciting and he'll need extra pilots as time goes on. It'd be daft to let myself get left behind.'

'Yes, he was telling me there'll be trips to the Continent and America. It sounds like a dream come true!' Sandie sipped her wine and thought of Denis, so cock-a-hoop at the thought of a trip to Guernsey. If it hadn't been for the pass he'd made at her she wouldn't be here now. She shut away once more the memory of the morning. Sky had just been trying it on, she told herself. He wouldn't do it again—she'd made it quite plain enough that she didn't want it.

And if Tim tried anything, it would be no more than a few kisses. He wouldn't try to force himself on her, and she knew that with him she'd be able to call a halt easily enough.

She had something to thank Denis for, Sandie thought in amusement. Maybe she'd send him a postcard one day—from one of those foreign trips. And wouldn't it be nice to see his face when he received it!

'You're not with me,' Tim accused and she came back guiltily to the present. 'You were miles away.'

'Sorry. I was thinking of those trips abroad. I wonder why Sky didn't mention them at beginning.'

'Wanted to be absolutely sure it was the ballooning you were interested in, and not the jollies,' Tim said sagely. 'It's going to be hard work, this job, and he didn't want anyone who was interested only in the foreign jaunts. Not that we aren't all looking forward to them—they'll be fun!'

'But haven't you already got a job?' Sandie remembered. 'In an estate agent's office, isn't it?'

'Mm.' Tim made a comical face. 'And every bit as fascinating as it sounds. Actually, I am qualified—but I'm waiting for stolid middle-age before I tie myself down permanently to that! No, I'm chucking it in and going full-time with Sky. I want a bit of interest before I settle down.'

'I can't imagine you ever being stolid,' Sandie smiled, looking at his twinkling brown eyes and cheerful round face. 'But I think I'd buy a second-hand house from you!'

'And that's one of the nicest compliments I've ever received,' Tim answered solemnly. Then his eyes went past Sandie to the door and his brows rose. 'Hal-*lo*. So this is why Sky didn't ask me to bring a girl. He knew the numbers would be even—and *how*.'

Sandie turned. She had been aware, with that prickling sixth sense that she seemed to have where Sky was concerned, that Sky had left the room some minutes earlier. Now he had returned—bringing with him a fourth dinner-guest.

Tim and Andy rose to their feet with one movement. All eyes were on the woman who had preceded Sky into the room—and, Sandie thought, with very good reason.

Almost as tall as Sky, with a statuesque figure that might have modelled for one of the more voluptuous sculptors, she could have stopped motorway traffic. Shining black hair fell in a heavy Cleopatra cut to her bare, creamy shoulders; eyes so dark that it was difficult to tell whether they were brown or blue glowed from an immaculately made-up oval face; the sumptuous curve

of swelling breasts showed above the low neckline of
the shimmering gold evening gown. The perfect skin
was set off by the glitter of what must surely be real
diamonds, and as she advanced into the room a drift of
expensive perfume scented the air.

Sky introduced them all, the woman smiling a faint
Mona Lisa smile as she acknowledged each greeting.
'And this is Sandie Lewis,' he said, drawing Sandie into
the stunned circle. 'My newest pilot. Sandie, this is
Wanda Tallon—a very close friend of mine.'

Almost mechanically, Sandie held out her hand.
Tallon was a good name, she thought irrelevantly,
noticing the long scarlet fingernails. The hand was cool
and limp in hers and she relinquished it with relief. All
at once, she felt drab and dowdy with her short jersey
dress, daytime make-up of lipstick and a flick of
powder, and unvarnished nails. Not that she'd have
used dark red anyway, she thought stoutly, seeing
Wanda Tallon's eyes flicker over her with an almost
visible mental shrug of dismissal.

'A *pilot*?' Wanda repeated, her husky voice amused.
'Do you mean in one of those *balloons*? Do you actually
*go up* in them—Cindy, was it?'

'Sandie. Short for Alexandra,' Sandie answered
shortly. 'Yes, I do fly balloons as a matter of fact. I
enjoy it. And I'm looking forward very much to flying
Sky's balloons.' She glanced at him and caught a twitch
of amusement on his face. 'Perhaps you ought to try it,
Miss Tallon, if you haven't already.'

A low throb of laughter. 'Certainly I haven't tried
it—much as Sky would like me to. No, If I leave the
ground it's in a proper aircraft—I couldn't trust *myself*
to a washing-basket, like a bundle of laundry!' Her look
implied that that was just what Sandie reminded her of.
'Not that they don't look very pretty, floating away up

into the air,' she continued, linking her arm through
Sky's. 'Just like a child, blowing enormous bubbles. But
*fly* in one—no, thank you!'

'You ought to have a talk with Mrs Collins,' Sandie
suggested demurely. 'You and she have a lot in
common.'

'Mrs *Collins*? Isn't that your housekeeper person,
Sky?' The tailored brows lifted. 'Whatever would I have
in common with *her*?'

'I've no idea,' Sky said hastily, with a forbidding
glance at Sandie. 'Unless it's an appreciation of fine
food. Because Mrs Collins certainly has that—as you're
about to find out. I believe dinner's ready at this very
moment.'

He turned towards the dining-room and the others
followed, seating themselves at the round table. Sandie
found herself between Tim and Andy, with Sky
opposite; Wanda was at his right hand and Andy's wife,
Su, at his left.

Maybe she'd better keep a low profile for the rest of
the evening, Sandie thought. Her sense of humour and
Sky's might match, but she had a shrewd idea that he
wouldn't appreciate any little quips directed at his
girlfriend. Flippancy, as Mike Dornley would have said,
was definitely out of place.

Which was a pity. Because when Sandie's heart was
as sore as it was now, flippancy was just about the only
defence she could manage. Without it, she might still be
driven to analysing her own feelings—and that was still
something she just didn't want to do.

# CHAPTER FIVE

SPRING drifted into summer. Sandie began work, attending the usual country shows—the larger ones, like the Three Counties, at Malvern, and the Royal at Stoneleigh in Warwickshire, and a good many smaller ones. She flew at gymkhanas, fetes and even, once, a rather smart garden party at a minor stately home. She flew at sports events, swimming galas and several ballooning events, when a whole cluster of balloons ranging from a dozen to over sixty would take off together in the pearly light of dawn, drifting away like confetti from a giant's wedding over the sleeping countryside.

It was, as she had expected, hard work. There was all the travelling for a start—one day she might be in Warwickshire, the next heading for Scotland, although Sky had, she knew, made considerable efforts to arrange dates geographically close wherever possible. There was the physical labour of loading and unloading the balloon in her trailer, though she had Tim and another ground crew member, Steve, to help her with that. But only Tim was experienced—Steve was a gawky seventeen-year-old who had been employed on trial, with the promise of a few trips and some tuition if he did well.

They saw Sky only occasionally, when he had time to leave London and attend a show somewhere within easy reach of the Cotswolds. He was quite impersonal on these visits, treating Sandie in the same way as he treated Tim and Steve, and she fought down her resentment, telling herself that this was what she'd wanted—to be treated as 'one of the boys'. No ladies in ballooning, she reminded herself fiercely, trying to forget the essentially feminine Wanda. It was quite obvious what kind of woman Sky preferred for his off-duty moments, and there was nothing Sandie could do to compete with that. Not that she wanted to! What Sky did with his time, who he spent it with, were completely without interest. Sandie had her job, and that was all she wanted.

All the same, when Sky departed in the evening with nothing more than a casual wave, presumably to drive back to his comfortable Cotswold home and spend the evening with the beautiful Cleopatra whom he described as a 'close friend', though she was obviously much more than that—Sandie could not help standing for a moment looking after him, a wistful ache in her heart. All she had to remember was one kiss. Imagination must supply all the rest.

But when she found her thoughts travelling in that direction, she jerked them to a violent halt and sent them on a different way. She just couldn't afford to think about Sky like that! The kiss itself had proved just how dangerous he was—dangerous to her. Sandie had long since come to terms with the fact that, much as she had tried to deny it even to herself, she had *enjoyed* that kiss. It had been different from any other kiss she had ever known, and its effect on her had been dramatic. That tingling thrill that had shaken her; the invading sweetness as his mouth played with hers. Another kiss like that, and she could be lost—and that was something that could not be allowed to happen.

No, it was better by far if Sky's and her paths didn't cross too much. Leave him to the sultry Wanda. She was happier with the uncomplicated comradeship of Tim and Steve.

Sky—what luck, she mused, to be given a name like Skyrrold, which could be so appropriately shortened. Almost as if his parents had known—but they couldn't have, for hot air ballooning hadn't become feasible until the late 1950s and had only become popular as a sport in the past twenty years or so, its real popularity growing in the last five. Still, it was rapidly taking hold now and the idea for using balloons to advertise was certainly catching on. Many pilots, unable to afford their own balloon, were eager to find sponsors who would pay either part or the whole of the cost in order to have their name displayed on a coloured sphere that would float across the countryside attracting attention wherever it went. Some companies even had balloons made in special shapes—there was the Robertsons' Golly, a huge doll that could not help but draw the eye as it drifted by, arms akimbo. There was a sparking plug, a bottle of wine, a gas flame—the list was growing, each new shape a challenge to makers like Mike, who employed skilled designers and engineers to work out the possibilities. With all these advances, it had been only a matter of time before an advertising company would decide to own its own fleet of balloons, and this was just what Sky Darrington, of Standish, Darrington and Bryce, had decided to do.

It was in the middle of August that the whole flight of balloons—six altogether—met at Bristol for one of the big events of the British ballooning year—the Balloon Fiesta. This was attended by balloonists from all over the world, and Sandie looked forward to it with some excitement. The event lasted for three days, with ballooning each morning and evening, and Sky was to be there too, with his own private balloon.

The morning dawned pale and glimmering, the grass of the sweeping parkland above Bristol shining with

dew. Sandie was there in the small caravan she used
when there was to be an early start, while Tim and
Steve slept in their own van. Quite a few of the other
balloonists did the same; they congregated together on
the previous evening, swapping stories and singing
songs, and Sandie went to bed feeling contented and
happy. She had met many old friends from her days of
ballooning with Con, made some new ones among her
fellow-pilots in Sky's 'stable', and she was looking
forward to the rest of the weekend. Sky had not
appeared yet, but she knew he would be there in the
morning and—she hoped—minus the stately Wanda.

She looked out into the grey light. It was barely five
but there were people already about, making coffee in
caravans or outside tents, checking their balloons,
towing the trailers on to the launching area. Each pitch
was marked, so that there would be no jostling for
position, and one or two eager souls had already begun
a preliminary inflation. With a shiver that was part-
cold, part-excitement, Sandie washed hastily and
scrambled into a scarlet tracksuit. It was part of her
regular ballooning outfit, matching the main shade on
the balloon, and its vibrant colour brought hidden
lights to her blonde hair and a sparkle to her eyes. She
flicked a brush through her hair, dashed bright lipstick
across her mouth, and was ready.

'Coffee!' she called to the other van, and Tim's head
emerged, still tousled. In a few minutes the two were
with her, gratefully sipping scalding mugs of coffee as
they went over their plans for the day.

'Tim can come with me this morning, and you this
evening, Steve. Luckily it's a perfect morning—if the
wind gets up during the day so that we can't fly in the
afternoon, you can come tomorrow instead. Mind how
you go in the chase—there'll be a lot of other cars on

the road and all looking for balloons! Did you say you had a friend coming today?'

'Mm. Guy from school. He can stay the whole weekend—sleep in the van with us.'

'That'll be a help. We really need four in the team, I must remember to tell Sky. What's this boy's name?'

'Bruce.'

'OK, well we'll give him a flight sometime during the weekend too. Now, there's nothing much going on during the day—no ballooning, I mean—but there's plenty to see here so once we're all back the day's free till four-thirty this afternoon. Launch is supposed to be at six, so there'll be plenty of time to get ourselves organised.'

A step sounded outside the caravan, and Sky's head appeared at the half-door. 'Hi. Any spare coffee?'

Sandie immediately felt herself blush. Cursing herself, she got up and busied herself pouring coffee. Oh, why did he have this effect on her? She had been fine all these weeks, barely seeing him—now, the sight of him and the prospect of a weekend in his company, had her trembling like a schoolgirl.

Sky came in and sat beside Tim, his eyes on Sandie's face. He accepted the coffee and watched her as she took her place opposite, next to Steve.

'Everything all right?' His voice was pleasant, casual, and Sandie bit her lip as she heard her own come out squeaky and high.

'Yes. Fine. We're all raring to go, aren't we?' She looked at the other two in appeal, willing them to say something to take Sky's attention off her.

'You're flying too, aren't you, Sky?' Tim asked, but Sky shook his head.

'Balloon got ripped last weekend. Stupid thing to happen, and I couldn't get it mended in time. Have to cadge a lift if I want to fly.' He kept his eyes on his coffee and Sandie prayed that neither of her crew would take the bait—for bait it undoubtedly was. But her hopes sank as Tim answered promptly: 'You can have my place, if you like. I was going up this morning, but it doesn't matter. It's a shame to come all this way and not fly.'

'That's kind of you, Tim, but it depends on the captain.' Sky lifted his brilliant eyes and let their gaze rest on Sandie's flushed face. 'What about it, pilot? Would you accept me as a crew member, in place of Tim?'

There really was not anything she could do about it. With a mutter that could mean anything, Sandie let it be understood that she would. Her delight in the morning had abruptly faded. After several weeks of keeping clear of Sky, avoiding both him and the memory of his lips on hers, she was now committed to at least an hour's flight with him—just the two of them, alone in mid-air. And she would have given a good deal for it to be otherwise.

Worries were forgotten, however, in the excitement of the launch. By six, all the balloons were in position on the field and spectators were beginning to arrive, gathering round the perimeter with cameras and binoculars. The ground was a patchwork of brilliant colour as a kaleidoscope of nylon was spread out and inflation began. Vivid hues billowed and fell, swelled again and surged into life. Here and there a balloon rose to hover upright, basket still on the ground, held just below the point of take-off. The colours and patterns were limitless—gaudy stripes of blue, green and red, flamboyant bands of black and gold. Some were chequered, others a glowing ball of only one shade.

Some had faces on them, a good many carried the names of their sponsors and symbols and logos that were instantly recognisable. A famous washing powder was represented, a brand of soft drinks, toys, books. The sight was arresting enough when the balloons were seen singly; *en masse*, like this, it was incredible.

Sky's balloon flight stood out from all the others, their brilliant scarlet like balls of flame against the clearing mist of dawn. Each one carried the banners that proclaimed which firm was sponsoring it; none of Sky's balloons were made for only one advertiser, the banners being interchangeable and easily replaced with a new addition to those who had decided that a balloon was a cheap and easy way to cry their wares. And the effect could be very widespread indeed; not only were balloons seen floating across the sky, they could appear in television items and even on personal photographs which might be shown or seen all over the country or, indeed, the world.

Sandie got her own balloon inflated early—she wanted to be in the air before the main body of the launch, so that she could look down on the mass of colour from above. Heart beating fast, she watched Sky leap into the basket with her, then concentrated on the launch. Hands-on—hands-off—it was exactly right. She gave a final roar of flame into the canopy, and they were away, climbing up through the crowded, swaying balloons, passing breath-takingly close to one or two—and then breaking clear, rising rapidly with just a handful of others, looking down over the edge of the basket to the rainbow throng below.

It was like a sea of multi-coloured foam, billowing, surging, the rounded crowns of the balloons like gigantic bubbles that broke away constantly, rising into the air with her, filling the sky with a floating mosaic of iridescent brilliance.

In a few moments, the scene had diminished. The park was an expanse of green, the colours of the remaining balloons a freckle of spattered colour on its surface. In the air, each balloon finding a different air-current, the spheres looked like baubles from a Christmas tree, shining in the rays of the early sun as they drifted quietly away from the commotion below and into the shimmering mist. Some were already little more than specks of brightness in the distance; others were close enough for the crews to call out to each other. Everywhere was the sense of tranquil harmony that Sandie had always associated with ballooning, the peace of the air in contrast to the hurly-burly of the earth, and when she turned and smiled at Sky her radiant face bore no trace of self-consciousness, no uncomfortable awareness of his dynamic personality. And when he drew her to him and kissed her, there was this time no terrifying racing of the blood, no frantic fluttering of the heart, only an overwhelming sense of rightness, of being in exactly the place she ought to be; in the basket of a balloon, suspended in her own private paradise between heaven and earth, and in Sky's arms.

They drew apart a little shakily, their eyes intent, only half-conscious of the cheers of nearby balloonists. Then Sandie remembered the burner and gave a hasty puff of heat into the envelope, while Sky turned and waved cheerfully to the pilot nearest him, who happened to be one of his own stable.

'Sorry, show over!' he called. 'That's as far as we can go just here—mustn't distract the pilot.' But below the edge of the basket, his hand found Sandie's and held it firm. And that, she found as she guided the balloon through the increasing warmth of the summer morning until they descended at last, their idyll at an end, was quite distraction enough.

It was at the end of the weekend, after the last flight on the Sunday evening, that Sky took Sandie out for dinner and told her that he wanted her to go on a special flight with him.

'What sort of flight? An advertising job?' Sandie paused, a spoonful of melon halfway to her mouth, wondering with sudden excitement whether it would mean a trip abroad.

'A sponsored flight, yes. It's for a health food manufacturer—a sort of play on sport, the light nature of balloons (getting at the slimmers, though I can't see that the shape's much encouragement!) and the fact that lightness uses—and therefore needs—less fuel, i.e. food. All very subtle. Anyway, they're having this special balloon made and I've got the contract to fly it, starting off with a flight across Wales. Starting at the coast and making use of the prevailing westerly winds, provided they co-operate, and hopefully landing at or near the factory, in the Midlands. Most of the planning's been done—it's been arranged for quite a while—but now my co-pilot's broken his leg and I'd like you to come instead.'

'Me?' Sandie stared at him. 'But why not one of the others? One of the men?' It didn't seem possible that Sky Darrington, woman-hater, could be asking *her* to accompany him on this trip. Not when he had so many others to choose from.

Sky said nothing for a moment or two. Then he said quietly, 'Never mind the others, Sandie. I'm asking you. Doesn't that speak for itself?'

Sandie felt a tide of colour creep up her neck and into her cheeks. No, she wanted to say, it does not. I still don't know whether you want me because I'm a good pilot—or because I'm me. And that's just what I *do* want to know. Because—because it's *important*.

And it was important, she knew, because she had at last, over this magical weekend, faced up to her feelings about Sky. It had been impossible not to do so, during that idyllic dawn flight, or during the ones that followed it; or during the long, sunlit days when there was little to do but wait for late afternoon, wandering around the exhibitions, lying on the scented grass, strolling through the trees in the hope of spotting the deer that roamed there. Yesterday afternoon they had explored Bristol, conjuring up the bustle of history along its ancient waterfront, tramping the decks of the first steamship, *Great Britain*. In the evening there had been a barbecue, finishing with a sing-song during which she and Sky had sat close together under the stars, vying with each other to remember the words of the songs. And today they had swum in a nearby pool, racing each other, playing silly games—and stopping every now and then to look at each other with dawning wonder, almost afraid to touch the moment unless like a bubble it should burst.

Sandie still didn't know how Sky felt—she dared not hope for too much. But she knew all too well now what her own feelings were. She loved him—loved him with all her heart and all her being. And if she hadn't loved him right from the start, she had known that it was going to come, this wonderful elation, this soaring delight. She had known that Sky held the power to take her heart away. And she had resisted it—because until then she had never given her heart to any man, and she was afraid of what might happen when she did.

'So you want me to come with you,' she said slowly. 'Do I have a choice? Or is it all part of the job?'

'It's part of the job, yes.' His eyes held hers, their blue the colour of his name, dark but bright. 'But you do have a choice. Making long flights wasn't part of your contract; if you prefer not to do it, you can say so.'

Sandie drew a deep breath. 'Then I'd like to come, please. I've never made a long flight before—so long as you understand that, I'd love to do it.'

'Good.' Their main course arrived and Sky sat back to allow the waiter to serve them with Dover sole and broccoli. 'And I'd love to have you along.'

After that shattering statement, he became entirely practical, discussing the arrangements that had been made, the logistics of the exercise, the time it was expected to take. By his standards, Sandie realised, it probably did not rate as a long flight at all—a trip across mid-Wales could not compare with the Pyrenees, or any of the other flights he had done. But Sky didn't seem to see it that way. Any flight was worth taking seriously—you could fall just as hard out of a balloon that had been up for only five minutes as you could after several hours. The length of time and distance meant extra precautions as far as fuel, food and drink were concerned, and a better ability to deal with weather conditions, which could change so drastically in mountain country. Apart from that, it was an ordinary flight—and that meant taking every care.

Sandie listened, aware that the weekend was catching up on her. She had had three days of early rising and late nights, with little rest in between. The plan, she remembered ruefully, had been to rest during the day— but with Sky there, seeming to want her company, she'd soon discarded that idea. Now, doing her best to discuss with some intelligence the special flight, she could hardly keep her eyes open, even after several cups of black coffee.

'You're just about dead on your feet,' Sky said abruptly, interrupting himself in the middle of a dissertation on food rations. 'Come on—I'll take you home.'

'Home!' Sandie giggled weakly. Home, tonight, was a small caravan in the middle of the park. Standing almost alone because nearly everyone else had left after the last flight that afternoon. Even Tim and Steve had departed, and suddenly she wasn't really all that keen on returning to the empty space that surrounded the little van.

Nor, it seemed, was Sky all that keen on leaving her. He glanced around at the moonlit emptiness, grunting to himself. Then he took the key from Sandie's fingers, unlocked the door and followed her in.

'I'm staying with you,' he said briefly. 'And you needn't look like that—you surely don't expect me to drive off and leave you all by yourself here, do you? Why in heaven's name didn't you tell me everyone else would have gone? I'd have booked you into my hotel. In fact, it might not be a bad idea to do that now.'

'Oh, no—you can't do that. It's far too late.' Sandie hesitated, looking at him through a haze of fatigue, conscious all the same of a stirring of excitement. 'Honestly, Sky, I'll be all right—I'll lock the door as soon as you've gone, and I'm sure——'

'I told you, I'm not going.' To her horror, he was shrugging off his jacket. 'Don't act the prim little miss with me, Sandie. I'm not going to force my attentions on you. I'm just going to lie down on this bunk and get a few hours' sleep. If you've got any sense at all, you'll do the same.'

He sat down on the bunk, bent forward to undo his shoelaces, then glanced up at her under long dark lashes. 'Don't just stand there, woman,' he said irritably, and she realised suddenly that he was tired too. 'Get yourself undressed and into bed. You can spare your maidenly blushes—I won't look. But you might remember that you've just agreed to spend two days in a small basket with me—there won't be room for modesty there, or hadn't you thought of that?'

Sandie's face burned as she watched him strip off his shirt and stretch out on the bunk, pulling over him a blanket that she had discarded the night before. Slowly, conscious of a sudden bitter disappointment, she undressed, and slipped into her own bunk. The romance of the weekend had melted like snow under a warm sun, and she wondered for a moment if it had ever really been. Had she imagined it all, that idyll which had begun with a kiss in the misty dawn? Or had Sky been playing his own particular game—softening her up, dissolving her antagonism, because he needed her for this particular flight? It probably meant quite a lot of money to him—the attempt would be televised, talked about in the papers, photographed for advertisements. The name of the health food manufacturer would become a household word—and Sky Darrington's balloon stable would receive a lot of publicity too. It was certain to bring more work his way.

As she fell asleep, Sandie wondered again just why he'd chosen her for this particular flight—and almost at once the answer slipped into her mind. How many of his other pilots, she mused, held a rating for night-flying?

It wasn't something everyone bothered with. And she wouldn't be surprised if the answer turned out to be none.

As if her body had become accustomed to awaking at

dawn, Sandie opened her eyes next morning just as the
first light began to filter in through the small windows.
At once she was tense, ready to leap out of bed—and
then she remembered that there was no flying today,
that there was no work at all until the next weekend,
and she relaxed. And then tensed again as she became
aware of something moving about the van and saw Sky
bending over her with a steaming china mug.

'Tea,' he said briefly. 'You were beginning to stir so I
reckoned you'd be awake soon. Feel better?'

'Better?' She struggled up and took the mug, sipping
it.

'You were pretty well shattered last night. I nearly
had to put you to bed myself! Matter of fact, I wasn't
much better either—I must admit I was quite glad to
crash out here instead of having to drive back to the
hotel.'

His eyes moved slowly over Sandie, and she realised
suddenly that she had undressed down to pants and bra
last night and that during her sleep the bra—not much
more than a wisp of lace—had lost its front fastening
and hung like a frail cobweb over her shoulders, hiding
nothing. Feeling a blush that started in her cheeks and
spread down to the white swell of her breasts, she pulled
the sheet up around her; but Sky bent forward and,
with one finger, drew it away again.

'Don't cover yourself up, Sandie,' he said softly.
'You're far too pretty a sight.' With gentle fingers, he
parted the lace and cupped her naked breasts in his
palms, looking down with an expression of tenderness.
Then a different expression came into his eyes; a
darkness that made Sandie's stomach twist and her
heart kick. And then the kick had become a wild gallop
as he bent and placed his lips on the full young curves,
gently at first and then with an almost involuntary

surge of passion, trailing a path of fire over her trembling skin as he gathered her into his arms. Sandie gasped and then heard herself groan. Somewhere, dimly, she had an idea that she ought to resist—ought to *want* to resist—but there was no will for resistance in her limbs. Instead, her whole body seemed directed, not towards submission, but towards a joyous participation, arching against him so that the breasts that still burned from his kisses were aroused even further by the roughness of the hair on his chest. She felt his lips at her throat now and her hands moved up to tangle in the thick golden hair as she stretched her head up and back, revelling in the sensation of his mouth on her taut skin. Then it travelled up, lingering in the hollow of her throat where the pulse beat like the wings of a wild bird, to the tip of her chin and thus to her own waiting lips.

'Sandie,' he muttered against her mouth. 'Sandie . . . Sandie . . . oh my God . . .'

With an impatient movement, he thrust aside the sheet that still came between them, staring down for a moment at the slender body in his arms. But Sandie wanted him closer; she reached up and pulled him down to her again, moving against him for the delicious friction of skin against skin, letting her hands roam his body as freely as his were moving over her, thrilling to his touch and knowing by his reactions that her own touch was equally arousing. He was on the bunk with her now, lying full length against her, lean and hard. Sandie let her legs twine with his, whimpering a little in her need, all her doubts forgotten in this whirl, this maelstrom of emotion that had her in its grip and would not let her go. She strained against him, wanting a fulfilment she scarcely understood, knowing that there could be only one end to this frenzied encounter. It had been inevitable from the first, she thought dazedly, and then thought fled as Sky placed one hand flat against her shoulder, keeping her pinned to the bed, and raised himself on one elbow.

His face was grave as he looked down at her. Sandie stared up, wondering why he had stopped, reaching out to draw him down again, arching herself so that the stiff and swollen tips of her breasts brushed against him. Desperately, she needed him to kiss her again; but instead of his lips, it was his finger that he placed against her mouth, and his eyes were sombre as a winter cloud as he watched her.

'Sky?' she whispered, a flicker of fear brushing her heart.

'I'm sorry, Sandie,' he said quietly. 'I didn't mean that to happen.' He stood up, thrusting one hand through the hair she had tousled in her fingers only seconds earlier. 'I thought I had more control.'

'More—control?' she faltered. 'I don't understand.'

'Don't you?' To her astonishment, his tone was almost savage. 'Don't you really understand, Sandie? You lie there, half-naked, flaunting all your very feminine attractions—and you say you don't understand? My God, what——'

'*Flaunting* myself?' Sandie broke in, her bewilderment turning to anger with a rapidity that shook her. 'How dare you? *I* never invited you to stay the night, Sky Darrington—and I certainly never invited you to start making passes at me again. In fact, I seem to remember telling you months ago not to touch me—or did you think that now I'm an employee of yours, that gave you some special kind of right? Of course, I do realise that this is *your* caravan, and that therefore you may feel that you have some say in what goes on in it—but I don't happen to share that——'

'Oh, for God's sake wrap it in, Sandie!' he cut in brusquely. 'All right, you've made it quite clear on more than one occasion that you don't welcome my advances. Or so you *say*. What happens when I do seems to belie that—or maybe it's a case of body and mind being in less than full agreement?' There was a sneer in his voice as he looked down at her. 'Only you know just what goes on in that innocent-looking blonde head of yours—but could it just be that you know yourself only too well? Know that you can't resist any man's touch? Is that it? Because you damned well can't resist mine, and you know it! And you're not above using that knowledge to torment me, are you?'

'*Torment* you? I don't know what you're talking about. All right, there does seem to be some kind of . . .' she drew a breath, 'physical attraction between us. But that's all. And I repeat, I'd rather you didn't touch me again. Sex without love doesn't happen to be on my list of desirable experiences—and you certainly don't love me!'

There was a moment's frozen silence while Sandie realised that she must have given herself away. Oh Lord, she thought miserably, why did I have to say *that*? Suddenly deflated, she pulled the sheet up to her chin, staring at the floor, unable to meet Sky's gaze.

'We'll leave it at that then,' he said stiffly, turning away. 'I did say I was sorry, but I don't think you noticed. I'll repeat it—there's nothing more I can do—and if you'll give me a few moments to go I'll be out of your way. I take it you can manage to hitch up the van?'

Sandie nodded, unable to trust herself to speak. The beautiful dream of only a few minutes ago had erupted around her in a volcano of fury and she felt drained and exhausted. So it was all over—the few moments of delirious joy that Sky felt about her just as she felt about him. She had been wrong, horribly wrong. He had merely responded as any man would, taking her nakedness as an invitation, natural animal passion taking over from rational thought.

Sky dressed quickly, ran a comb through his hair, and unlocked the door of the caravan. He turned briefly at the door and their eyes met and held; a mute appeal in Sandie's, an unfathomable expression deep in his.

'I'll be seeing you,' he said curtly. 'I'll be in touch about the trans-Wales flight when I've got some more details worked out.'

Sandie stared at him. 'You—you mean it's still on?' She felt dazed, uncertain.

'Did I say it wasn't?' His tone was crisp, as if she were nothing more than an employee. 'The fact still remains that you're one of my pilots and I want you to do this particular job. I've told you I won't touch you again, if that's what you're worried about.' He stepped out into the early morning mist and closed the door behind him.

Sandie sank back on to her bunk, her mind reeling. He still wanted her to fly with him—but did *she* want to fly with him? It didn't seem to have occurred to him that *her* feelings might have changed!

But even as she thought that, she knew that they hadn't. Sky Darrington might see her as nothing more than a desirable body, to be taken and enjoyed—but her feelings towards him were much, much deeper than that. The love that she had acknowledged only a few days ago ran deep and strong through her, like a subterranean river through hard rock. She couldn't let him make love to her again—the pain of knowing it meant little or nothing to him would be too great. But apart from that, she knew she would do whatever he asked of her. Including making a balloon trip across Wales.

Including making a balloon trip to the moon, if that was what he wanted.

# CHAPTER SIX

THE balloon for the special flight was the biggest Sandie had ever flown. It stood tall above the launching ground, a deep burgundy red, its basket crammed with fuel cylinders; with each one lasting no more than an hour, they were almost more important than the two pilots. Sandie eyed the tiny space left, into which she and Sky must fit. There certainly wouldn't be much room to manoeuvre, she thought wryly, and hoped that he would stick to his promise not to touch her. Though surely he would; flying this monster of a balloon was going to take all their concentration particularly as they would be crossing difficult terrain.

'This isn't going to be the flight itself,' Sky had explained when he'd outlined his plans. 'Just a practice run. We aren't trying to break any records anyway—just provide a few interesting pictures and TV, and a story. It's really publicity for the balloon as much as anything—people will look out for it with all the more interest when they've seen it on TV, doing this, and therefore the sponsor's name will become more firmly fixed in their minds. They're going to use the balloon as their trademark, so the pictures will be appearing on a whole range of goods.'

Sandie nodded. So this flight was not in itself going to attract much notice. There would be no stewards or observers this time, no TV cameras other than those at the start and finish. On the flight proper, they would be accompanied by helicopters—keeping at a safe distance she hoped!—which would film them on all stages of

the flight. There would be other balloons too, Sky had
said, with photographers aboard, and a big reception at
the other end. But this flight was more of a
reconnaissance, a dry run, and there were only a few
people present at the launch.

It didn't make Sandie feel any better when one of
those people turned out to be Wanda Tallon.

She must have arrived during the inflation for she
certainly hadn't been present when Sandie had glanced
around to see the TV crew setting up their cameras. It
was practice for them too, she supposed, the only
rehearsal they would get, and she was glad of the
chance to get used to them. Any self-consciousness
would spoil the whole enterprise on the day itself. But
she had soon forgotten it as she busied herself with the
inflation, holding open the mouth of the envelope as
Tim directed the fan into it, blasting air in so that the
deep red nylon struggled into life and billowed out on
the silvery grass. The sponsor's name began to take
shape on the stitched panels, pale blue against the rich
burgundy, and the giant sphere slowly rose as Sky
began to direct flame in to heat the air now trapped
inside.

'I must admit they do look rather beautiful,' a husky
voice drawled, and Sandie looked round with a start to
see Wanda standing close behind her. The older woman
looked as immaculately-groomed as she had done on
the night that Sandie had met her in Sky's house.
Dressed in a jumpsuit of a deep red that exactly
matched the colour of the balloon, she looked like some
exotic creature from space-fiction—much more appropriate to fly in the balloon than me, Sandie thought
ruefully, aware that already her fair hair was tangled
and her own red tracksuit was too bright and clashed
with the balloon's darker colour. Perhaps she could do

something about that before the actual flight—it would
certainly look more effective. Although she would never
look as dramatic as Wanda, with her glossy black
Cleopatra hairstyle and her brilliant violet eyes. But
there wasn't time to think about that now, although
Wanda didn't appear to appreciate that for she was
now approaching the basket where Sky was busy
checking the karabiners and the burner.

'Hello, darling.' Her cooing voice carried quite clearly
over the still grass and Sandie saw the rest of the crew
look round and grin. There was not one of them who
would not have liked that greeting directed at him, she
thought a little sourly, and wondered how Sky was
taking it. He did not generally thank people for
interrupting his pre-flight checks, but this time he
glanced up and gave Wanda that smile of his—the one
that never failed to catch at Sandie's heart. He hadn't
smiled at her like that since the Fiesta, she thought
miserably, and knew again that ache that had tormented
her ever since that last morning.

'All ready for the great adventure?' Wanda was
asking in that low voice that seemed to invest every
word with hidden meaning. 'Do you know, I almost
wish I were coming with you—*almost*.' Her throaty
chuckle indicated that he was not to take this seriously.
'But I must say I'm a touch worried about little Sandie.
Don't you really think it would have been better to
have had one of the *men* with you on such a long trip?'

'Not much choice, I'm afraid,' Sky answered briefly,
still making his checks. 'Guy I did want hurt himself,
and Sandie's the only other one with sufficient
experience.' He didn't make it sound as if he was
exactly thrilled to have her along, Sandie thought
ruefully. And if he had to have a woman, there could
not be much doubt that Wanda would have been his

first choice—if *she* had had the experience. No doubt she had plenty of experience in other directions!

'Well, enjoy yourself anyway,' Wanda told him, as if she thought he would probably find it difficult considering the company he was in. 'I'll be waiting at the other end with champagne! And then we'll have that luxury weekend we've been promising ourselves. That'll be something for you to look forward to.'

'Oh, I'll look forward to the finish all right,' Sky said enigmatically. 'Ready, Sandie?' Hop aboard—I think there's *just* room for you in here!' Sandie scrambled in beside him, hoping that she wouldn't get cramp so hemmed in by fuel cylinders. 'Right—we're off.'

'Take care, darling.' Wanda leaned into the basket and kissed Sky on the mouth, a lingering kiss that left nobody in any doubt as to their relationship. 'I'll be following in the car—but I promise I'll be at the other end first!' She threw Sandie a casual glance. 'Lucky I'm not the jealous type,' she said lightly, 'or I might be quite concerned about Sky flying off into the blue with another woman! But I don't think I have too much to worry about where you're concerned, do I, sweet?'

Sandie was fortunately saved from having to answer this; even as Wanda finished speaking, the balloon was in the air, rising steadily above the heads of the little knot of spectators. Wanda was little more than a bright speck on the dew-misted grass, staring up at them, eyes dark shadows in her pale creamy face. And then it was impossible even to see that much. There was just a spatter of moving figures down there, like ants running on the ground. They were too tiny to look at any more and Sandie breathed a sigh of relief and turned her attention to the scenery.

The flight hadn't been an easy one to plan, covering as it did the mountainous country of Wales. But Sky had worked out a possible route (wind and weather permitting) which would take them over very scenic— and therefore photogenic—country, ideal for the sponsor's purpose. He had considered the two different approaches to mountain flying—the use of the complex low-level currents, the turbulence caused by wind-flow on the slopes and the thermals and drainage caused by sun-warmed or shaded mountainsides, all of which could be difficult and dangerous but provide spectacular close views; or the more cautious approach, climbing much higher and swooping over the peaks with several thousand feet to spare. The views then were equally spectacular but more distant, and although Sky's had to be the last word, he wanted to take into account his sponsor's requirements.

'We'll take the high-level approach this morning, I think,' he told Sandie as they left the launching-site far below. 'You've got that camera, have you? You can take some pictures to show them, give them an idea of what it'll look like. We'll drop lower later on, when we've crossed the highest parts.'

Sandie watched eagerly as the mountainous country- side unfolded like a contoured map beneath her. They were to fly over Plynlimon, the vast high plateau on which the Rivers Wye and Severn were born; she unfolded her own map, identifying the features as they appeared—Pen Plynlimon Fawr, the highest point where Owen Glendower must once have stood as he planned his raids on the English; Devil's Bridge, with its leaping waterfalls and gorges and, as they headed east, the two rivers, starting so near yet quickly diverging before their long journeys to the estuary where they meet again. Then the expanse of the plateau, green and brown, merged into a muted carpet as the balloon lifted higher. The view was wide now on all sides and, now that the early morning mist had dispersed, sharply clear so that Sandie could pick out the jutting peaks of Snowdonia to the north and the mellower lines of the Black Mountains to the south, and the view became so vast that she found it difficult to identify the different peaks. Remembering her camera, she began to take photographs, wishing that there could have been snow to make it all the more spectacular.

She mentioned this thought to Sky, who nodded agreement. 'It might be a good idea to save the actual flight until later, when we'd have snow,' he said thoughtfully. 'It certainly would add to the filming if these mountains were white instead of that rather sombre darkness of the rock and peat.'

'It would be magical,' Sandie said simply, and he gave her a quick grin that lifted her heart. All at once, everything was all right between them. They were a team, working together on something they both loved and understood, and the bond strengthened and grew tighter between them.

The morning passed without incident. Occasionally they caught sight of the twisting mountain road that the chase cars would be using, but there was seldom a sight of vehicles, although Sky had his binoculars. Somewhere down there, Tim and Steve and, Sandie supposed, Wanda would be looking up, hoping for a glimpse of them. The TV crew, too, would be wanting to get shots of them in the sky; although this wasn't the actual flight, any footage might well be used in the final film. But if they were there, the two people who drifted high above the mountains in their crowded wicker basket never saw them. They were quite alone above that quiet yet savage landscape, floating in a world of silence accompanied only by the occasional coughing raven or soaring kite.

They changed cylinders several times, keeping a careful eye on how the fuel reserves were holding out. It was important, Sandie knew, to land with a good reserve, even though the chase car carried sufficient replacement cylinders for the rest of their flight next day. She knew, too, that by the time they landed late this evening—perhaps after dark—they would both have had quite enough of the cramped space in the basket, surrounded by empty cylinders which they would gladly have jettisoned had it not been dangerous and, in any case, illegal to do so. Long flights were certainly tests of endurance, and Sandie was glad of the exercises that Sky had evolved to prevent muscles becoming too cramped as they stood together in the confined space.

'I don't like the look of that cloud formation,' he remarked later, glancing back behind them. They were somewhere over Radnor Forest now, a stretch of wild, open moorland purple with heather, with the odd farmhouse tucked into a valley below, reached by narrow tracks. Sandie turned and followed Sky's frowning glance. She bit her lip—the clouds were obviously a front, a heavy darkness that was approaching quickly from the coast. They spelled wind and rain—conditions that, for ballooning, were far from ideal.

'The weather forecast never mentioned *that*,' she said, and Sky shrugged his agreement.

'Too right they didn't—we wouldn't be up here now if they had. Well, I don't much fancy flying in whatever they're going to hand us—we'd better think about putting down.'

Sandie sighed with disappointment. The flight had been going so well—she and Sky had established a rapport that had warmed her heart, and she had a nasty feeling that it might fade once they were back on earth. But she knew he was right; to stay in the air now would be to court disaster, and the front was gaining on them fast. Already she could feel the coldness of the air that preceded it, and the first gust of wind would not be far behind. She glanced up anxiously at the towering canopy, looking to see if there were any distortion of the shape that would tell them the wind was already blowing against the envelope, but there was none, and to her relief the flame of the burner was still straight as Sky gave a burst of heat. But that could change with dangerous rapidity. There was no time to lose, and they both began to peer downwards, looking for a good landing-spot near the road, where the chase car would be able to find them or they might at least be able to reach a telephone.

Descent could not be achieved quickly, however. They had been flying high and Sky did not approve of rapid descents, especially at the end of the afternoon when there might be thermals or turbulence to contend with. The layers of air-currents they would pass through on their way down might each present a different problem; it was better to enter each one slowly, so as to deal with various conditions. At the same time, they were still drifting, and as the only way to steer the balloon was to use the air-currents, these had to be studied carefully during the descent.

'What's that main road?' Sky asked, and Sandie frowned at the map.

'The A483. Can we land somewhere near it?' On either side of the road the land rose in high, rolling moors populated mostly by sheep. Not very pleasant country to have to carry a heavy basket and balloon and all those cylinders. She watched anxiously as the road ribboned along beneath them. Sky opened the parachute a fraction to assist the descent, but a swifter air-current caught them and they swooped across the road and left it behind.

'Damn! No, we can't land near it.' He looked back at the bank of clouds; they had obscurred the sun now and were drawing inexorably nearer. 'And I don't think we can make it across that ridge to the next—that would be the Knighton road, wouldn't it? I'm afraid I'll just have to put down wherever I can. Any sign of the chase car?'

'None at all,' Sandie said gloomily. 'I haven't seen them for a long time. I hope nothing's happened to them.'

'Don't suppose it has. They probably decided to have a picnic in the hills.' Sky spoke grimly and Sandie understood his annoyance—the chase car ought to have had them in sight as much as possible from the very start. 'Well, we're going down now. Prepare for a few bumps—God knows what the terrains's like under all that heather.'

Quickly, he carried out the pre-landing manoeuvres, switching to a full fuel cylinder, making sure that rip and valve lines were at hand, seeing that Sandie had made all loose equipment, such as the camera and food packages, secure. The balloon was now descending fairly rapidly, levelling off less than a yard from the purple tips of the heather. Sandie braced herself for impact, hoping that there were no large rocks lurking under the amethyst carpet. She watched intently as the heather drew nearer—a foot nearer, two feet nearer, inches . . . and then, with only a slight bump after all, they were down. Sky vented the parachute opening just enough to keep the balloon from taking off again, and they looked at each other and grinned with relief.

'Well, we're down and the balloon's OK,' Sky

remarked. 'The question now is how long we can keep it up as a marker before that front gets to us.'

'Not long, by the speed of its approach,' Sandie said, watching the threatening dark line. 'There must be quite a wind driving that lot across.'

'Mm.' Sky frowned. 'I think you're right. That's a pretty bad storm, and it could be upon us in less than half an hour. I think we'd better forget about marking our position and get the envelope packed away.' He glanced around at the featureless moor. 'It's a bloody nuisance—they'll never find us here, don't even know where to start looking. We'll have to go for help ourselves.' He pulled the red line and the balloon began to deflate, collapsing behind them in a long red streamer like a trail of blood. 'OK, Sandie, you can get out now—I'll get the lines unfastened.'

Sandie scrambled out, her legs weak and stiff after the long hours in the basket. But there wasn't time to worry about that. The balloon was the most important thing now, and she began to work her way down from crown to mouth, squashing out the air that was still trapped inside, folding it in and rolling it tightly to make a package that would fit into the canvas bag which they had carried with them in the basket. After a few minutes Sky came to join her and they worked together, racing against time to get the envelope safely stowed away before the rain began.

'Not that it would be a disaster if it did get wet,' Sky commented, 'but I'd rather it didn't. About the only way to get a balloon dry is to inflate and fly it again— and we don't know when we'll be able to do that. If it hadn't been for this storm, we could have waited until morning and then taken off to finish the run—but if it hadn't been for the storm, we wouldn't have landed! So we'd better pack it away, I don't want it going mouldy.'

Sandie didn't answer. She knew most of what Sky was saying already, but she was aware that he was talking mainly to allay his own feelings of disappointment. He just needed a sounding-board, and if she could be nothing else to him—she still had not forgotten that lingering, intimate kiss Wanda had given him just before take-off—she could be that. She shoved the last scrap of protruding nylon into the bag and stood up painfully.

'Now what? We ought to try to get the whole thing under cover.'

'Did you see anything as we came down?' Sky asked, and Sandie's forehead creased.

'There was something a bit further over—an old house or barn, I think. One of those derelict farms like we saw earlier, perhaps.'

'How far away?' The clouds were very near now, their edge a sharp contrast with the blue of the sky. The air was noticeably colder and a chilly wind ruffled Sandie's hair.

'About a mile, I should say.' Sandie dragged her pack of maps from the basket, found the right sheet and unfolded it. 'I think we're here—on Pool Hill. See, there's a track going down to the source of the River Lugg, and then down to the main road at Lloiney. I should think the building was beside that track. Probably this one—Beacon Lodge.'

Sky frowned at it. 'If we're on Pool Hill, our shortest way back to civilisation would be straight down to Llanfair Waterdine. Going the other way, we're veering in a circle.'

'I know—but we'll never make Llanfair Waterdine, carrying the balloon, before dark. I don't think we'd even make it on our own. And we can't possibly carry it all in one go.' Sandie pushed a grubby hand through

her hair, leaving muddy streaks among the pale
strands. 'At least there might be some shelter at this
place.'

'Yes.' The first heavy drops of rain spattered on their
heads. 'Well, we don't seem to have much choice. OK
Sandie, get all the things we can't carry at once into a
pile and cover them over. Better get your own
waterproofs on and we'll carry the balloon between us,
then come back for the rest. All right?' He dragged on
his own anorak and waterproof trousers, then pushed
one hand through the rope loops on the bulging canvas.
'Here we go.'

The journeys that they made back and forth to the
derelict farm, carrying balloon, basket, burners and
loose equipment all in turn, merged for Sandie into an
apparently endless tramp across the increasingly wet
moors. Fortunately, once they had traversed the first
fifty yards or so of tall, clinging heather they found
themselves on a clear track that led, as the map showed,
to the fallen buildings. But it was hard, grinding work
and after the long hours already spent in the balloon—
was it really only that morning that they had set off in
such promising sunshine?—it was exhausting. By the
time they made the last trip, Sandie was wet through in
spite of her protective clothing, her hair was straggling
into her eyes and her legs felt like lumps of particularly
heavy and unco-operative lead.

'Well, that's it.' Sky had dropped the last bundle on
the floor of the only weatherproof room they had
found, and looked around. 'Not a palace exactly, but
dry, even if we do have to share it with a flock of
sheep.' He moved his foot, clearing the floor. 'Or what
they've left behind them, anyway.' The sheep, smelling
of damp wool and uttering grumbling bleats, had
moved out when Sky and Sandie had first appeared,

and although they still stood disconsolately around the
door hadn't ventured in again. It was obvious however,
that they had been in occupation for some time, and
Sandie looked round in a kind of mute despair,
knowing that she would never be able to rest here yet
knowing too that there was nowhere else to go.

It was almost dark now, the rain falling steadily. She
stood quite still in the middle of the crumbling room,
shivering with cold, and put a shaking hand to her face.
Now that the effort was all over, she felt sick and faint
with reaction, and when Sky glanced down at her and
moved closer, she went into his arms as if it was the
only place she wanted to be, burying her face against
his shoulder.

'Hey, don't give way now,' he said softly. 'You've
done a fantastic job. Everything's all right now.'

'Is it?' She lifted a weary, dirt-streaked face, eyes
huge grey shadows in the dusk. 'What do we do now?
We *can't* stay here—it's horrible. And it's miles to the
nearest road, all across the moors, we'd get lost if we
tried. And——'

'Hey!' he said again, and his voice was so gentle that
she wanted to cry. 'You know your trouble—you're
cold and you're hungry. Look, it's not so bad. I can get
rid of most of this dung the sheep have left—it's dry
and it doesn't really smell so bad. And there's plenty of
air coming in! And when I've done that, I'll make a
fire—we've got our matches and there's a load of wood
from the lath and plaster ceilings, and beams, we can
have a really good blaze. That'll make everything seem
better. We can strip off these wet clothes and dry them,
and we can eat some of the food we've got with us.
Don't worry, Sandie—everything's going to be all
right.' He touched her cheek very gently with the tip of
one finger. 'You take this big torch and collect up some

wood while I clean the floor a bit, all right? Once we get a fire going and have something to eat and drink, everything will look a whole lot better, you'll see.'

Will I? Sandie wondered as she did as she was told, moving automatically and more because she hadn't the strength to argue than because she believed him. Depression made her lethargic, but by the time Sky had cleaned the floor she had managed to collect quite a sizeable bundle of thin laths and some bigger beams, rotten and dry, which Sky built up into a pyramid in the old fireplace. She watched apathetically as he put a match to the splintered laths; but with the first tiny flame that licked up through the pyre a tiny flicker of hope stirred within her and as the fire took hold and the laths burned with a heat that soon caught at the time-softened beams, she felt an answering warmth beginning to comfort her chilled, damp body.

Maybe Sky was right, she thought, bending to rummage for some food in her pack. Maybe it wasn't so bad, after all.

An hour later, Sandie sat before the fire, wrapped in one of the blankets that had been stowed in the basket in case of accidents. It was surprising, she thought, just how much they *had* managed to stow aboard, considering the problems of space and weight, with fuel being of prime importance. But the two space blankets, thin enough to take up very little room but warmly insulating when unpacked, had been considered a possible lifesaver. And so, she thought, they had proved.

She had been reluctant to comply when Sky had first ordered her to strip off her clothes. The comradeship they had enjoyed all day receded as she looked doubtfully at him, thinking uneasily of how far they were from civilisation, how trapped she was in this derelict farmhouse with him, with the rain and wind beating at the tumbledown walls. But Sky had reacted with impatience, telling her not to be a fool.

'You'll catch pneumonia if you stay in those clothes all night,' he told her roughly. 'But that's up to you—I can't force you, and I've no intention of stripping you myself. God knows what hysterical scene you'd create if I did! Do what you like—*I'm* going to strip off, and if you don't like it there are plenty of other rooms in the place!'

Not rainproof rooms, Sandie thought, knowing that he was well aware of this fact. She hesitated. What he said made sense and he had already begun to carry out his intention, peeling off the dripping anorak and waterproof trousers. Underneath, his corduroys were sodden and as Sandie watched he began to fumble with the belt, glancing up as he did so to catch her eyes on him.

'It isn't a peepshow,' he pointed out coolly, fingers still moving. 'Not that I mind you looking in the least— but it's hardly fair if you don't entertain me as well!'

Blushing deeply, Sandie hastily turned away. She had to admit he was right—she was shivering violently now, the heat from the fire producing only an unpleasant humidity inside her clothes. Taking a deep breath, she began to take off her own things, telling herself as she did so that he was right, she was being silly. After all, he had seen her virtually naked before now hadn't he? She tried to close her mind to what had happened then. It wasn't likely to happen again here—not in these spartan and still somewhat squalid surroundings. Quickly, before she could change her mind, she stripped down to bra and pants, then reached for the blanket to cover herself before taking them off too. She held the clothes in her hand, uncertain what to do with them. They were all as sodden as if she had been thrown into a lake.

'Here—let me hang them up.' Sky was behind her, taking the soggy bundle from her hands. Slowly, she turned. He had doubled his blanket and fastened it about his waist. He had also rigged up a primitive clothes-horse on the other side of the fire and already hung his own things there. He did the same with Sandie's, then came back to her.

'We'll keep warmer if we sit close together,' he said matter-of-factly. 'Now for some food. Wasn't there a flask of hot soup? I wonder if it still is! And there were some cold sausages, if I remember rightly—we could toast them again over the fire. You know, this is really quite fun. I told you—there's nothing like being warm and dry for making you feel better.'

Efficiently, he found and poured out the soup then impaled the sausages on sticks and held them over the glowing fire. Sandie sipped up the lukewarm liquid and did begin to feel better. She moved a little closer, watching the light of the flames play on the muscles of his chest and shoulders, glinting on the blonde hairs, rippling as he moved. The planes of his face were thrown into sharp relief; not smooth and godlike, like Denis's too good-looking features, but almost harsh, the line of the jaw uncompromisingly firm. There was a faint golden stubble showing on his chin; he hadn't shaved since very early that morning and a beard was beginning to grow. She wondered idly what he would look like with a beard. A handsome Scandinavian, she guessed, or, going further back, a magnificent Viking . . .

'Sausage,' Sky's voice interrupted her reverie as he held a pointed stick towards her. Sandie jerked back

from some Nordic saga to the derelict farm and took
the sausage hastily, squealing as it burned her fingers.
But the first bite was good, the spicy heat warming her
blood, and she took the next as eagerly, though with
more caution, then refused any more. Sky must be even
hungrier than she and there were sandwiches and rolls
to fill up the corners. There was chocolate too, and
between them they demolished a large bar, settling back
with little sighs of contentment when it was all gone.

'Not a bad meal. I feel ready to tackle the world
again now.' Sky listened for a moment to the drumming
rain. 'Not until the morning, though! I'll kill those
weather forecasters.'

'So much for fine settled weather,' Sandie agreed
sleepily, and she felt Sky's arm come round her.

'You're dead beat. Lean against me and try to get
some sleep.' His voice was gentle, comforting, and she
knew that tonight she had nothing to fear from him.
With a little sigh, she turned her face into his shoulder,
savouring the clean sharp scent of maleness. She would
not sleep, she thought, but it was pleasant just to sit
here, cuddled close and feeling the regular beat of his
heart against her cheek, the warmth of his skin against
her face. The golden hairs tickled her gently, but she
didn't want to move. She didn't want to do anything
but sit here, close against him, throughout the rest of
the dark, stormy night. If she had nothing else, she
thought hazily, she would have this to remember. And
somehow—tired as she was—she wouldn't fall asleep.
Somehow, she would stay awake—so as not to miss one
single, precious second of it . . .

At some point during the night, the rain must have
stopped and the wind died down. It was still cold, but
light was filtering through the creeper-hung doorway

when Sandie awoke and lifted her head to stare dazedly around her.

Somehow, during the night, she had slipped down to lie close against Sky's body. And somehow the two blankets had got wrapped around them both, enclosing them in a warm cocoon. As she stirred, she could feel his legs, warm and hard, against hers, his muscular thighs, flat stomach and broad chest in contact with her at every point. And her face flamed as she realised that they were both quite naked and that she couldn't possibly move without waking him.

There had been another morning when they had awoken together, she remembered, and neither had she forgotten what had happened. It had ended with angry words, insults and recriminations. She didn't want those now; these moments were too precious. She had lost the night, the hours she had intended to spend awake savouring Sky's nearness. Soon, he would wake and then she would have to move quickly to prevent a repetition of what had happened on that other occasion—but until then, couldn't she just pretend? Pretend that their closeness had come about from desire rather than necessity; pretend that they were lovers, waking after a night spent together in sweet, tender passion, with perhaps more passion to come; pretend that Sky loved her as she loved him, deeply and wholly and with complete commitment . . .

With a tiny whimper she settled closer, letting her body move against his in languorous capitulation. A small voice told her that this would do no good, that it would only make her feel more bereft when he woke and rejected her—or, worse still, took her from simple lust—but the temptation was too strong. She wanted desperately to feel that hard body against hers, twine her legs with his, let her softness merge with his hardness until the yearning in her could pulse its way to the climax it needed so much. She wanted his lips on hers; wanted to feel his exploration of her body, his final triumphant discovery, wanted to make her own demands and have them fulfilled. Her heart thundered in her breast as her movements began to be answered by his. Still sleeping, he was beginning to respond, an exquisitely dangerous response that could soon take charge and overwhelm her with its strength and irresistible force. An irresistible force, yes ... but there was no immoveable object here, she thought hazily as Sky's lips moved round to hers and she gave herself up to his kiss. She was ready to move in just whatever way he wanted her to, and now the warning voice was unheard as their two bodies came together as naturally and easily as if it had always been meant to happen. As perhaps it had, Sandie reflected in those last lucid moments before thought evaporated and the processes of the body took over in a wild frenzy of delighted ecstasy. Perhaps it had always been meant to happen; perhaps there had never been any escaping it; perhaps it would have been useless to try any longer.

Whatever the truth, it was too late now. And she flung herself back on the hard ground, receiving Sky's body into hers with a soaring certainty that this was the right, the only thing that could have happened. And that, whatever else might happen, she would never forget it. Never; never; never ...

# CHAPTER SEVEN

THE storm had completely passed over during the night, and Sandie woke to find the sun across her face in a shifting pattern as it filtered through the ivy that hung over the sagging door. For a few moments she lay dazed, staring in bewilderment at the two sheep who were gazing in with equal wonder; then her memory of the night flooded back, and with it a surge of warmth and tingling happiness.

She turned on her side, reaching out for Sky, expecting to be gathered into his arms. But the space beside her was empty, though the warmth of the insulating covers told her that he had only just left her. Her joy dimmed a little by disappointment, she hesitated, then smiled to herself and settled back. He would be returning soon, she told herself confidently, and then—well, then perhaps they would make love again . . .

Her body shivered involuntarily as she thought over the way he had held and kissed her, the slow caressing of his sensitive fingers, the roughness of his hair-covered chest against hers, the smoothness of his thighs. Closing her eyes, she let herself experience again the mounting crescendo, the thundering climax of their lovemaking. She sighed a little, moving her body with reminiscent languor, feeling the invading softness that had welcomed his passionate demands. 'Sky,' she whispered on a breath of desire, 'oh, Sky . . .'

'Here I am.' His voice cut into her thoughts almost crudely, startling her. Her eyes flew open and she stared

up, noticing at once with a sharp dismay that he was
dressed, alert and strangely detached. His eyes looked
down at her, but there was no answering desire in them;
simply a matter-of-fact objectivity, as if he were
assessing her ability to get up and cook breakfast.
Feeling somehow rejected, Sandie automatically pulled
the thin space blanket up to her chin and looked up
with wide green eyes.

'I've just been down to the farm,' Sky continued in
that cool, detached voice. 'It's only about a mile away.
I've rung the location number—apparently the chase
car was involved in an accident soon after the launch
yesterday. No, nobody was hurt ...' in answer to
Sandie's immediately anxious exclamation, 'but the
vehicles were damaged and there was a long delay while
they got help and hired new ones. In the meantime, of
course, they lost all track of us and never managed to
get a sighting again. They'll be out here as soon as
possible, and you'll be glad to hear that they can get a
Land-Rover all the way up here from the farm, so we
won't have to do any heavy lugging of balloon and
basket. All we have to do is sit tight and wait.'

He paused, and his eyes darkened. Almost reluctantly,
he knelt beside the makeshift bed and with one
forefinger traced the line of Sandie's cheek. She closed
her eyes, feeling the tremor shake her body, feeling his
delicate touch like a thin line of fire, and her face lifted,
turning into his palm to kiss the hollow.

'About last night,' Sky said quietly. 'I didn't mean it
to happen, you know.'

'I'm glad it did,' she whispered, opening her eyes
again for her glance to meet his, grey-green merging
with dark sapphire. 'I—I've never done it before, Sky.'

'No, I realised that.' He smiled. 'Not because you
weren't any good at it! But you have that lovely fresh

innocence, Sandie, a kind of wonder that's rare these days. It's a very long time since I've met that.'

His words reminded her sharply of Wanda. There was no wondering innocence about her, Sandie was quite sure. Wanda, glossy and glittering would be very experienced indeed—as would any other girl-friend that Sky had. Rare as her own reactions might be, a man like Sky would very soon tire of them. Freshness could easily become gaucheness, innocence be seen as immaturity. Was this what he was telling her?

'Sky——' she began, but he interrupted her sharply and a second later she understood why. Sounds from outside announced the approach of several people, and as Sky uncoiled himself and went over to the door Sandie looked frantically around for her clothes. If that was the ground crew, she didn't want to be found stark naked—particularly if Wanda were with them!

But when she had scrambled hurriedly into still-damp underclothes and tracksuit and gone outside, she found that it wasn't the ground crew at all. They were on their way, the smiling Welsh farmer assured the two balloonists, but meanwhile why not come down to the farm and have breakfast? He had the Land-Rover outside, look, and the wife was busy cooking and they could be down there in a few minutes. And their friends would have to come up through the farmyard, so what was the point of waiting here?

'Your old balloon will be all right just where it is,' he went on, 'but we can put some of your stuff in the Land-Rover. Just push it in anyhow—it's starving you are, I'm sure.'

He was right there, Sandie agreed, but the breakfast his rosy, cheerful wife provided soon cured that. And by the time the ground crew arrived, she and Sky were sitting back in the big kitchen, warmed by a huge Aga cooker, finishing up a pile of hot Welsh cakes and emptying a vast pot of tea for the third time.

'Pity we didn't know about you last night,' the farmer observed, watching them benignly as he might have watched a pair of rescued lambs. 'You could have been down here in the warm, in a comfortable bed, instead of up there in that old house. Bet it was a long, cold night, wasn't it? And in that storm and all—yes, it's a pity you didn't find your way down here.'

Sandie glanced across under her lashes at Sky, wondering if he was thinking the same as she. Yes, they might well have been here, warm and dry in a comfortable bed—or beds, more likely. But she knew where she would rather have spent the night. The magic of being in Sky's arms, united with him in a rapture that took them higher than any balloon, was more than compensation for a hard floor, a draughty and derelict house and a violent storm outside. It was something she would never forget, always hold precious, even if Sky did afterwards return to the sophisticated Wanda.

At that moment they heard the growl of a Land-Rover churning up the steep track to the farm. They jumped up and made for the door, emerging in time to see the ground crew occupying a Land-Rover and a large van, just about to enter the farmyard.

'Rescue at last,' Sky observed, and went forward to greet them. And as Sandie followed, she saw that among them, still managing to look immaculate and extremely sexy in slim-fitting black sweater and slacks, was Wanda Tallon. Not that Wanda noticed her—she was too occupied with throwing her arms around Sky's neck, kissing him thoroughly, and linking her arm possessively in his as the others crowded round to hear the balloonists' story and tell their own.

It was painfully obvious to Sandie that Sky didn't at

all object to this enthusiastic and proprietorial greeting.
In fact, she thought sadly, he seemed to be enjoying it.
And he didn't once look around to see how *she* was.

Last night—the night he 'hadn't meant to happen'—
was clearly no more to Sky Darrington than a pleasant
interlude.

The entire crew and the farmer went up to the derelict
house together to collect the balloon and the rest of the
equipment. At first, efforts had been made by the
farmer's wife to get 'these two poor girls' to stay behind
in comfort; but Sandie, knowing that Sky would expect
her to take her share of the work and responsibility,
refused to be cosseted. And Wanda had clearly had
enough of letting Sandie share too much of Sky's
company. Since hearing that they had spent the night
together in the ruined house, her attitude had changed,
narrow-eyed suspicion taking the place of casual
dismissiveness. Wanda saw everyone in her own terms,
Sandie thought. She wouldn't have missed such an
opportunity and she did not expect anyone else to. The
fact that she was right to be suspicious didn't really
help!

'No, of course I'll come too,' Wanda cooed. 'I can
cheer you on, if nothing else. And to be quite honest,
Sky, I've been surprised at how worried I've been about
you! I know you're a big, grown-up man and able to
look after yourself—but not knowing where you might
be, lost out here with only little Sandie—well, *anything*
could have happened.'

'Well, it didn't,' Sky answered, completely missing
her insinuation—or maybe he was just pretending to!
'Sandie and I both survived very well, as you can see.
But come along by all means, Wanda, if you want to.
It's a beautiful morning up on the moors. In fact,

there's no reason now that the weather's cleared why we shouldn't set off and finish the trip.'

'*Finish* it?' Wanda repeated, aghast, and he nodded.

'Why not? The weather's good, there's nothing wrong with the balloon, you're here so you can follow us—successfully, this time, we hope—why should we abandon it? We're supposed to be rehearsing a two-day flight, after all. The only snag is we're making a later start than we planned, but that needn't be too much of a problem.'

Wanda shrugged her slim shoulders. 'Well, it's for you to say, Sky. You'll do what you want, no matter what I say.' She glanced at Sandie, a quick shot of venom that startled her. 'So you'll be having another nice long day with Sky after all,' she remarked silkily. 'Isn't that nice!'

Sandie opened her mouth, but before she could answer, Sky cut in, his voice suddenly hard.

'No, you're wrong there, Wanda. Sandie won't be coming with me this trip. I'm taking Tim instead.' He didn't look at Sandie as he spoke. 'All right, Tim? You're ready, are you?'

The young balloonist threw a quick glance at Sandie, his face pink with embarrassment. 'Yes—yes, of course I'm ready,' he stammered. 'But—but I thought the idea was to see if Sandie could manage—I mean——' He floundered to a stop, his face agonised, while Sandie tried desperately to control her thumping heart and suddenly ragged breathing.

'I know Sandie can manage,' Sky said, still in that hard voice, 'but she's not coming with me today. Yesterday and last night were enough for her to cope with when it's only a rehearsal. I'm sorry, Sandie——' for the first time, he spoke directly to her '—but this time I don't want you along.'

Sandie found her voice at last. 'Don't want me along?' she exclaimed, her voice rising. '*Don't want me along?* Just what are you saying, Sky Darrington? That I can't cope with a long flight and a—a night's camping?' The memory of what sort of night it had really been caught at her memory, bringing a stinging scarlet to her cheeks. 'Are you afraid I'll do something stupid—fall asleep, drop out of the basket or something? Because if you are, why not say so? And if you're not—well, just what *is* your reason? Because I can manage perfectly well, I can fly for as long and as far as you, if I'm given a chance!'

'I've no doubt you can,' Sky said patiently, 'but I——'

'Then why won't you *let* me?' Oblivious of the watching faces, Sandie faced him, fists clenched, eyes blazing. 'What's suddenly wrong with me that you don't want me any more?' She was painfully conscious of the double meaning behind her words and wondered briefly if he was too. Surely he must be—surely he couldn't reject her now. 'Please,' she begged him, subduing all her more rebellious instincts in her efforts to persuade. 'Please let me come now. It's been arranged all along. Why change everything?'

For what seemed eternity but must have been only seconds, their eyes met and held. Sandie felt that her whole heart must have been in the look she gave him then, in that despairing plea that he should accept her, not just for her ballooning but for what had been between them during that dark, storm-ridden night. But after a tiny flash of communication that was too brief to identify, Sky's glance was veiled. It was as if they had never met, or were at best casual acquaintances. And then he turned away and she knew that there was no use in further appeal.

'You're being selfish, Sandie,' he said curtly as he began to examine the basket. 'Tim needs these hours to obtain his licence. You'll be on the final flight, don't worry—all being well.' He glanced around at the silent group. 'Well, get with it, everyone. I'm starting inflation. We've wasted enough time this morning.'

Sandie turned away, sick at heart. There were enough people to help with inflation, she thought, but she didn't want to be accused of sulking so she made her way to the other end of the balloon to handle the crown rope. With practised ease, almost without thinking, she held on to the end, leaning back on the taut line as the balloon took shape and rose slowly into the air, then moving in towards it and finally, as she felt the first indication that her feet might leave the ground, letting go.

The morning which had started with such joy and warmth had turned sour. For some reason which was inexplicable to her, Sky had rejected her, making it clear that he didn't want a moment more of her company than he had to suffer, particularly on a long balloon flight when they would be isolated from all other people, alone in a world that had become theirs and was now forbidden her.

Why? What had she done? Was it because Wanda had arrived on the scene with her sophistication, her uninhibited kisses, her air of possessiveness? Had Sky suddenly felt remorse, a regret at having been unfaithful to his current mistress?

Or had he, on seeing the older girl again, realised as Sandie had feared, that innocence and freshness could soon pall beside experience and maturity? Had he decided that another day in a balloon with Sandie would be nothing but boredom—especially if Sandie now looked upon him as her own lover, her own private property.

Well, he needn't worry about that, she thought as she sat silently in the crowded Land-Rover as it bumped down the moorland track, past the farmhouse and out to the main road. Sandie Lewis had never yet run after any man. She wasn't about to start now, with a man who didn't want her—no matter how much she might love him.

A girl had to have some pride, after all—didn't she?

The rest of the day dragged by like a leaden-footed centipede. As chase car, they had to keep an eye on the balloon whenever possible and follow it, trying to predict on the map just which direction it might take and where it might land. On a normal flight, lasting only an hour or so, this was relatively easy, though snags could occur, but on a long flight it was much more difficult. They were all tired by the end of the afternoon, and inclined to be snappy.

'We couldn't even stop for lunch,' Wanda grumbled as they threaded their way through heavy Midland traffic. 'There was that nice little pub, just right—I'm sure it wouldn't have mattered if we'd stopped there for half an hour.'

'Balloons don't stop for lunch,' Sandie reminded her. 'And it would have been more like an hour. We could have lost sight of it altogether, and it's no fun having to put down with no ground-crew.'

Wanda shrugged. Since Sandie had joined the chase cars, she had clearly lost some interest in when and where the balloon came down. It would land somewhere, sometime, and then she would be able to have Sky to herself again. Meanwhile, he was safe enough up there with Tim and Sandie was trapped below. As long as Sky and Sandie were separated, Wanda was happy. Though she would, it was clear, have been even happier if she hadn't had to spend the waiting time in Sandie's company herself!

'Do you think Sky really will let you do the actual filmed flight with him?' she inquired casually as they waited in a lay-by to see which direction the balloon, drifting high above them now, would take. The men had got out and were standing by the roadside, talking and laughing. Sandie wished she had got out too, but she couldn't let Wanda's question go unanswered.

'Of course he will,' she said shortly. 'It's all arranged.'

'But it was arranged that you'd do all of this one, wasn't it?' Wanda was deliberately needling her, she thought angrily. 'He could change his mind again—take Tim with him.'

'Tim's not a qualified pilot.' She was uneasily aware, though, that he very soon could be. After today, he would have more than enough hours in his log book. He only needed to take his written examination and do one flight with an examiner. . . . Was that what Sky had in mind? To get Tim qualified quickly, so that *he* could do the flight?

'Well, I'm sure Sky must have had a reason for taking him,' Wanda remarked. 'He doesn't do many things without good reason.'

Like making love to virgins on Welsh hillsides, Sandie thought wryly. Had he had a good reason—like he loved her? She knew the answer must be no. But Sky wouldn't need that as a reason—just wanting her, finding her attractive, that would be enough. And finding her willing too, she reminded herself. He had never tried to force her—as Denis had. He'd never needed to . . .

'You never actually said what happened last night,' Wanda went on, watching her closely. 'After you landed, I mean.'

'There isn't much to tell.' Sandie was aware of her glowing cheeks and knew that there was nothing she could do about them. 'We just got everything as much under cover as we could, lit a fire with old wood from the house, and waited for morning. What else could we do?'

'Oh, quite a lot. At least, I should have thought so.' Wanda studied Sandie's burning face. 'But perhaps not, in your case. You really are quite old-fashioned, aren't you? All Victorian principles and strait-laced morals. Or at least, that's the impression you like to give, isn't it? I wonder if it's the truth.'

'Well, that's something you're not likely to find out, isn't it?' Sandie said as lightly as she could manage, and Wanda smiled, a curving cat-like smile.

'I wouldn't be too sure of that,' she murmured. 'Sky and I are very close, you know. We tell each other most things. And if anything *did* happen between you last night—well, I won't lose too much sleep over it myself. He's only human, after all, and you're obviously crazy about him.' The smile faded, leaving her narrow-eyed and venomous. 'But don't run away with the idea that it will ever happen again, little Sandie Lewis. Or that it meant anything. Because it didn't, I can tell you that for free. If Sky Darrington filled in the long cold night by amusing himself with you, then that's all it was— amusement. Because Sky belongs to *me*. And whatever he may get up to now, he knows as well as I do that once we're married it will stop. Understand that, little flying girl? There's no future for you with Sky, none at all. Except as a pilot. And any funny business on your part, and you won't even be that—so be warned.'

There was no time for Sandie to answer. The men had returned and were climbing back into the Land-Rover. The balloon had taken a course that could now be predicted and it looked as though it might be landing fairly soon. The long day spent in trailing the country roads, trying to follow the elusive globe, was coming to an end.

Sandie could not have been more thankful. It seemed a very long time since she had woken that morning and she was aware of a heavy, exhausted misery. If she could have opted out of the reception committee now, she would have done so. She was not at all sure that she ever wanted to see Sky again.

And she certainly was not sure that he would want to see her.

The shrilling complaints of the telephone split the air of Sandie's tiny flat and she turned over irritably, aware that if it went on much longer she would just have to answer it. It had woken her from the sleep she had at last managed to fall into and she wished heartily that she had taken the 'phone off the hook before going to bed. After all, she might have known it would start again today; it had rung on and off for most of the previous evening, and although she'd ignored it then she'd known that if the persistent caller tried again she would have to give in.

Wearily, she slid out of bed and padded over to the table. The telephone screamed at her once more before she picked it up; then there was blessed silence and she was tempted just to lay it gently on the table and go back to bed. But a kind of masochism made her lift the receiver to her ear and speak.

'Sandie?' Sky's voice said, as she'd known it would. 'Is that you? Where in hell have you been?'

'Here and there,' she answered coolly. 'Why?'

'Why? Why what?'

'Why do you want to know? Sky, I do have a life

of my own,' she said, thinking *and that's a lie*. 'I'm
not on duty again until Wednesday. Is there any
reason why I shouldn't go out or even away, if I
want to?'

'No reason at all, except that I've been trying to get
you for three days now and I don't believe you *have*
been away. You've been there, haven't you—if not all
the time, for a good part of it. And you've just refused
to answer the 'phone.'

'That's my privilege too,' Sandie said stiffly,
miserably aware that this wasn't at all the kind of
conversation she wanted to have with Sky. 'You can
choose when or if to ring me up—I can choose when *or
if* to answer.'

She heard his sigh of exasperation. 'Sandie, this isn't
getting us anywhere——'

'Do we want to get somewhere?'

'Well, I thought we did! Obviously I was wrong.
Look——' She could almost see him restrain himself,
keeping a control he found difficult '—we've got to talk.
There are all sorts of things we have to discuss——'

'Such as?' It was no use—she couldn't afford to let
him get under her guard again. Once that happened,
she'd be totally lost. So far, she was managing, even if
refusing to answer the 'phone and spending most of her
time curled up in an armchair staring into space was
not her normal way of life. But on that level, she could
cope. Let Sky Darrington get through to her again with
his slow, devastating smile, his heavy-lidded, brilliant
eyes and his thrilling and sensitive touch, and she'd
have no defences.

Again that sigh, and this time when he spoke his
voice was tight with control.

'You know perfectly well we need to discuss the
Welsh flight,' he told her. 'Apart from other things to

do with the job. And——'

'I'm still on that flight, then?' Sandie interrupted.
'You haven't decided to take Tim?'

'No, of course I haven't decided to take Tim!' The
control was snapping now. 'There was never any
question of taking Tim. I merely wanted to give him
more flying hours, and since you were obviousy tired
it seemed the natural thing to do. Tim still won't be
as experienced as you are, even when he's taken his
exam.'

'Not in ballooning, anyway,' Sandie said, and could
have bitten out her tongue. There was a very dead
silence.

'And just what is that supposed to mean?' Sky
inquired at last, his voice like ice.

'Nothing. It was just a stupid remark.' Sandie ran her
fingers through her hair. 'Sky, I haven't been feeling too
bright—could we leave this discussion for a few days?
There's no hurry, is there? I——'

'You're not well?' His voice changed sharply and she
cursed herself. 'What's the matter?'

'Nothing. Nothing at all. I'm just—tired, I suppose.
A bit down. I'll be all right by Wednesday, don't worry.
I'd just rather be on my own.'

'Well, in my opinion you've been on your own long
enough,' he said crisply. 'Stay where you are. I'm
coming over.' And she heard the 'phone go down with a
decisive click.

Sandie groaned and replaced her own receiver. Now
she'd done it—he could be over at her flat within a
quarter of an hour, far too soon for her to get dressed
and make her escape. Anyway, she didn't really have
the energy to do anything about it. The apathetic
exhaustion that seemed to have swamped her ever since
the end of the Wales–Midlands flight seemed to fill her

limbs with lead, and her mind moved sluggishly. She would have to see him soon anyway, so why not get it over with? Though she hadn't the least idea of what to say to him.

Moving slowly, she washed and dressed herself in sweater and jeans. Her fine hair seemed to have lost its silkiness, she noticed, and her jeans were definitely looser than they had been a week ago. A summer spent in the open air had made sure that her face was tanned, but it had lost that healthy golden glow and now looked merely dingy.

Well, what did it matter? Sky had made it quite plain that what she looked like was immaterial to him. And if he hadn't, Wanda's words hadn't left any room for doubt. The night they had spent together in the derelict farmhouse on the hills had been just an amusement for Sky, nothing more. And if she had any sense at all, she'd pretend that it had been the same for her.

Well, she'd certainly tried. When the balloon had finally landed, the ground crew had been there on the spot to meet it, and Sandie had been able to busy herself with the deflation, keeping well out of Sky's way. She'd caught a curious glance coming from him once or twice, but he hadn't come close enough to speak—and when he'd looked as if he might, she'd turned quickly to Tim, bestowing on him her most dazzling smile, and asked him how he'd enjoyed the flight.

'Oh, fantastic,' Tim answered with enthusiasm. 'Thanks for standing down, Sandie. It was absolutely great—I learned a lot and I've got all my flying hours now, ready for the exam. Sky says that if I can pass it soon he'll give me the next balloon!'

'That's marvellous,' Sandie said, wondering if Sky meant to buy more balloons or whether she would find herself redundant now that he looked like acquiring another male pilot. Tim gave her a conspiratorial grin.

'Only snag is, I won't be working with you,' he whispered. 'And I thought we were evolving such a beautiful friendship, too!'

Sandie smiled. She would be sorry, too, to lose Tim as part of her crew. They got along so well—he was open, uncomplicated, friendly and always cheerful, finding fun in anything but particularly when things began to go wrong. And although he had made no secret of the fact that he found Sandie attractive, he had never tried to force himself upon her. There had been times, indeed, when her affection for him had been so warm that she'd wondered if it might develop into something more. She knew it could easily happen on Tim's side. But, fond though she was of him, she knew that there could never be that essential spark between them—that spark that flashed between her and Sky like a high-voltage current, leaving her weak and trembling and longing for nothing else than to be in his arms.

The spark seemed to have burned itself out now though, she thought ruefully as she finished stowing the balloon into its bag and saw Sky talking to Wanda. As usual, the older girl had her arm linked in his and was gazing up into his eyes, one slim hand smoothing back her ebony hair. Sky was paying a good deal of attention to her, Sandie noted with a twinge—looking down at the creamy face, totally absorbed, listening and nodding. Probably they were discussing that luxury weekend Wanda had mentioned. Or perhaps even their marriage . . .

When Sky had finally come over towards Sandie, she had made up her mind to behave as if the night before had been no more for her than it had been for him—time-killing amusement. She gave him a bright, brittle smile, caught the flicker in his eyes and congratulated herself. Maybe he'd wanted her to fall at his feet, she thought—well, that was something she'd *never* do!

'All right, Sandie?' he asked quietly, and she nodded quickly.

'Yes, I'm fine. Any reason why I shouldn't be?'

'No, of course not. You just seemed a bit—well, quiet.' His cobalt eyes searched her face. 'You're quite sure?'

'I told you, I'm fine.' Sandie glanced at her watch. 'I'd just like to be away soon, there's something I want to do this evening.'

'But you're coming to have a meal with us all—it's all laid on—you knew it was arranged.' He was beginning to look puzzled.

'No, I don't think I will, thank you,' she said briskly. 'As I said, there are several things I need to do and tonight would be a good time——'

'You're not sulking because I took Tim?' he said sharply, and Sandie looked at him with wide-eyed surprise.

'Of course not. I'm glad he had the chance. Sky, I do have other things to do, that's all. Do you mind?' She glanced across at Wanda, ostensibly talking with one of the others but watching them like a cat through slitted eyes. 'You won't be lonely, I'm sure.'

She'd walked away then, needing all her strength of mind to do so. And she had not seen Sky since; nor, for the past two days, had she answered the telephone, knowing that it might be him.

And now he was coming to see her. Would be here at any moment. Her heart started jumping as she stared into the mirror at the thin, sallow face and the huge, anxious eyes. What would he say when he saw her? What would *she* say? What was going to happen?

There was one small crumb of comfort. He certainly wouldn't find her attractive, looking as she did now. And that was just as well—because if he touched her, she knew she would be totally unable to resist.

She heard the sound of the front door opening and closing. Footsteps on the stairs. A pause, outside her door; and then, as she closed her eyes, feeling suddenly sick, a firm knock.

Moving like an automaton, Sandie reached the door. Her hands shook as she opened it, and she looked up at Sky with unconscious appeal, begging him silently not to add to her burden of despair, not to be harsh or unforgiving. Not that she was quite sure what he had to forgive—but one quick glance at the stern lines of that craggy face told her that *he* knew. Her heart sinking even further, she stood back for him to come in. There was no point in doing anything else—he quite clearly intended to come in, whether she wanted him to or not.

'And now,' he said, his voice as cold as frozen steel, 'maybe you'd like to tell me what this is all about.'

# CHAPTER EIGHT

SANDIE backed away from him as he advanced into the room. He looked bigger than ever in this tiny space, his whole bearing terrifyingly formidable. Fearfully, she raised her eyes to his face, quaking at the set implacability of his granite features, casting about for some means of escape but knowing there was none.

'Sky,' she began, her voice trembling. 'Sky, don't ...' She had reached the table, she realised in dismay, and her hands caught at it as Sky came even nearer, so near that she could feel the warmth of his body through her thin shirt and her breasts brushed against the rock of his chest.

'Don't what?' he asked menacingly. 'Don't hurt you? Don't shout at you? Or—don't kiss you?'

His voice softened at the last words, but the menace was still there and Sandie closed her eyes, almost too frightened to speak. Just what she was frightened of, she could not really have said—a moment's thought would have told her that Sky was not the kind of man to physically abuse a woman. At least—she didn't think he was. Nevertheless, he spelt danger loud and clear. And Sandie would have given a good deal to have had something she could protect herself with—preferably something hard and businesslike.

'Is that what you're afraid of, Sandie?' Sky went on, his voice little more than a gentle murmur and as terrifying as a snarl. He lifted one hand and touched her chin with the tip of one finger. 'Are you afraid I'm going to kiss you again? Make love to you? Just as we

135

did up on Radnor Forest that night, with no one to hear our cries but the sheep? Is that what you're afraid of—that you'll forget all your maidenly inhibitions again, just as you did then, and actually *enjoy* being a woman? Was it so very dreadful?'

He lifted her chin so that she was forced to meet his eyes, burning like blue flame into her mind. Dreadful? she wanted to repeat. No, it wasn't dreadful at all—it was heaven, paradise, and I want it again more than I want anything. But I daren't. Just now, I could perhaps break free of the spell you've cast over me—but if I lay in your arms once more, there would be no chance. No chance at all . . .

And if Sky really had been just amusing himself with her—if he really did look on her as a last fling, a last amusing episode before he married Wanda—well, it could mean only one thing for Sandie. Disaster.

'Well?' Sky persisted, his finger leaving her chin to trail down her neck and into the collar of her shirt. '*Was* it so dreadful? Is that why you've been hiding yourself away? Or maybe it wasn't dreadful at all. Maybe you *did* enjoy being a woman. Maybe you'd like to repeat the experience.'

Sandie twisted herself away from him, taking advantage of his relaxed posture to slip past him and make for the door. But Sky was, as always, too quick for her. Stretching out one hand as she went past, he caught her, almost lazily, and held her in a grip she had no hope of breaking. Pulling ineffectually at his iron fingers, Sandie felt her fear evaporate in a frenzy of anger, and she flung her head back and glared at him, eyes blazing green as a cat's.

'What's all this about enjoying being a woman?' she demanded hotly. 'What makes you think I *don't* enjoy being a woman? Just because I don't jump into bed

with every Tom, Dick and Harry who comes along—
does that disqualify me, or something? Oh, I know you
enjoy being a *man*—you prove it, don't you, over and
over again with any woman who happens to be willing?
But I don't have to prove anything, Sky Darrington—
not to you, not to myself, not to anybody else. Yes, I
enjoy being a woman—but I don't have to sleep with a
man to enjoy it. There are other ways.'

'Really? You amaze me.' Sky drew her to him,
ignoring her struggles. 'Such as what? You must admit,
you don't make many concessions to your sex. You
shorten your name until it sounds like a boy's, you do a
job that's mostly done by men, you wear jeans most of
the time, you don't bother much about make-up—all
right, maybe you don't have to *prove* you're a
woman—' he let his glance slide up and down her
rounded figure '—anyone can see it. But you don't seem
to *enjoy* it much.'

'And just how would you know that?' Sandie
inquired coldly, though inside she was almost weeping
with hurt. 'The only kind of woman you acknowledge is
the sleek and sophisticated type—the glamour queen,
wrapped in furs and dripping with jewellery. I don't
happen to be that type—and there are other kinds of
woman, you know. You just haven't noticed them
around. Because really and truly, you don't like women,
do you? You need them—you need them to admire you
and look up to you, you need them to take around with
you so that you can feel good and so that no one will
guess your secret. You need them to make love to—to
*amuse* yourself with. But you don't really *like* them.
You've never bothered to look at any woman to see
what's really there, under the skin. You just choose a
pretty ornament, a plaything other men will envy you
for. That's why you don't see me as a woman—because

I'm ordinary and not glamorous, and because I don't swoon all over you or say the things you want to hear.' She paused, hardly able to believe that she was talking in this way to Sky. 'All the same, I'd swear I'm more of a woman than your glamorous cut-out of a beauty queen. I'm *real*, Sky—flesh and blood, full of failings, stupid sometimes, wrong sometimes. But real. *Real*.' Suddenly she had run out of things to say. She stared up at him for what seemed a long time, emerald eyes locking with sapphire, and then she felt desperately tired. 'Let me go, Sky,' she said quietly, and as his hand released her wrist she turned away and sank down on a chair, elbows on the table, forehead leaning against her palms.

The silence was so long that she began to wonder if he'd gone. Why had she bothered? she wondered dully. None of what she'd said would make sense to him. It barely made sense to her. All that about being real— what had she meant by it? Dimly, she knew that she'd put her finger on a deep truth about Sky, but she could not have explained it. If he asked her what she'd been talking about, she would just have to shake her head.

But Sky didn't ask her anything. Instead, she felt him move away from her, heard his footsteps cross the room. There was the sound of cupboard doors being opened, a kettle being filled. Dazed, she only half-listened. The strain of the last few days had left her feeling depressed and empty, and the tormented conversation had completed her despair. More than anything else, she wanted to crawl into bed, turn her face to the wall and let everything slide away into oblivion.

'Here,' Sky's voice said, quite close to her again. 'Tea. It'll do you good.'

He lifted her head, holding it gently in his hands, and cradled her against him. Sandie felt a few weak tears

slip from her eyes and track slowly down her cheeks.
Still holding her against him, Sky lifted the cup and
brought it to her lips, and Sandie sipped and swallowed
obediently.

'That's better,' he said quietly. 'Now hold it yourself,
and drink it.' And when she had finished and set down
the cup, feeling better already, he went on, still quietly,
but with a grim note back in his voice. 'And just how
long is it since you ate or drank anything?'

'I—I'm not sure. This morning—yesterday? Not long
ago, anyway.'

'Not long ago? An earwig crawled out of that teapot
when I rinsed it! Sandie, you're an idiot. You've just let
everything go—and why? Tell me.'

She shook her head. 'I can't . . .'

'You can, and will.' He dragged another chair over
and sat in it, looking intently at her, keeping her face
turned towards his with a firm hand. 'You were all right
on the flight we did. What went wrong? Was it because
I took Tim with me the second time—or was it because
of what happened in that old house? You've got to tell
me, Sandie.'

'Why?' she asked with a faint return of spirit. 'Why
have I got to tell you? What good will it do?'

'I don't know that it *will* do any good,' he said
quietly. 'That depends on your answer. But I've a right
to know, can't you see that? It's obviously something
that concerns me—and if I've hurt or upset you in any
way, I have to know. So that I have a chance at least to
make amends.'

'Amends?' Sandie echoed dully. 'And just what sort
of amends can you make?'

'I can't know that until you tell me,' he returned with
a touch of exasperation. 'Sandie, for God's sake stop
beating about the bush. Let's get to the root of it.'

Sandie bit her lip and stared at the floor. How could she tell him the truth—that she loved him, was pretty sure she would always love him? There was no hope for her—he was going to marry Wanda. Whether or not he loved the other girl seemed immaterial. He wouldn't ever love Sandie, that was what mattered. So there was no point at all in telling him.

'Was it because I took Tim in the balloon?' he asked, and she looked helplessly into his face. If she said yes, what would he think of her? He would think she was selfish, inconsiderate, uncaring, and he'd be right. Did she really want him to think that of her?

'Was it because of what happened between us?' he went on. 'It was your first time, wasn't it, Sandie? Did I hurt you in any way—upset you? Have I spoiled it for you?'

'No!' she cried, unable to restrain herself. 'No, you haven't—it was wonderf——' She stopped abruptly, covering her face again. She hadn't meant to say that—but she could not deny the most rapturous and exciting experience of her life. It would be denying herself as well as Sky, and she just couldn't do that. 'No,' she said in a whisper, 'you haven't spoiled it for me.'

And then it seemed unnecessary to say any more. Sky's eyes darkened to a deep navy as she looked at him, and he reached out his arms to her. Without even thinking, Sandie went into them like a child. Her own arms went around the lean, muscular body and she felt a great sigh escape—whether from him or from herself she could not tell. He drew her head down on his chest and buried his face in her soft hair.

'Thank God for that,' he muttered huskily. 'I was afraid—God, I was so afraid! But it's all right, Sandie? It really is all right.'

He was holding her so tightly that she could barely

move, but the tiny nod she managed seemed to satisfy him and he drew her closer still, his fingers tense against her neck. His lips were on her face, in her hair, moving to find her own mouth, and she raised her face to his, lips parted in readiness. Their kiss was like a taste of honey, sweetness and strength combined, soft and pure as nature yet with a potential ferocity that had her shaking. Her senses faded under its power, and she clung to Sky, whimpering somewhere deep inside, wanting the moment to go on for ever yet knowing that she could not tolerate much more of the intense ecstasy it brought.

It seemed an eternity before either of them moved. Then Sky ended the kiss and drew away slightly, looking down at her with eyes that were hazed with passion. He shook his head slightly, then ran a hand through his corn-blond hair and grinned shakily.

'You know something?' he said. 'I'm as bad as you are—I've hardly eaten for three days either. And I have a feeling we could both use a good square meal—if only to give us strength to continue this—er—conversation later. What do you say, Sandie? Will you come out and have dinner with me?'

Sandie glanced down at herself. 'I'll have to change. I look terrible.'

'Not to me,' he said softly. 'To me, you look wonderful—but if you want to change, you go ahead. Only—don't be too long, all right?'

Sandie went through to her bedroom, still dazed by the turn taken by events. A few hours—minutes?—ago, she was in despair, believing that Sky cared nothing for her, that he was promised to Wanda and there could be no hope of any relationship between them other than that of employer and employee—unless she was willing to be a plaything for spare moments. Which she wasn't.

But now—she saw again that look in his eyes, felt the pressure of his hands on her body, the warmth of his skin against hers. How everything was different.

He still, observed that aggravating little voice inside her which always seemed to see everything so clearly, hadn't actually *said* anything. Like he loved her— wanted to marry her—anything positive. And a tiny chill touched her at the thought. But she quickly brushed it away. He didn't *need* to say anything. Not when he looked at her like that—touched her like that. Kissed her like that.

There were times when words just weren't needed at all. Times when they would have been nothing more than an intrusion.


Sandie could never remember afterwards what they ate that night. It could have been manna from heaven, the fruits of paradise—or it could have been fish and chips or beans on toast. Whatever it was, she ate it with her eyes on Sky's face, drowning in the tenderness of his looks. Whatever wine she drunk—whether it was finest champagne or cheapest 'plonk'—it tasted like nectar. And the light-headed joy she felt had little to do with its alcohol content. That too came directly from Sky; from the dark night-blue of his eyes, from the sweetness of his smile, from the gentleness of his hand as it touched hers.

She could not remember either what they had talked about. About themselves—about ballooning? She couldn't tell. Perhaps they did not talk at all, just communicated with their eyes. Perhaps their emotions were so deep that they shared a kind of telepathy, a knowledge of each other's minds that went far beyond normal expression and could not be described.

Sandie only knew that as Sky took her home that evening she was filled with a deeper, more joyous contentment than she had ever known existed. She knew that as he took her to the door of her flat nothing could ever again come between them, nothing spoil this deep rapport. She knew that there was now no hurry, no urgency in their love. It was there for the taking, whenever they wanted it, whenever the right moment arose. And if that moment lay in the future rather than now—well, that was fine.

'I won't come in,' Sky said as if answering her thoughts. 'You're exhausted and we both need time— time to absorb what's happened.' He took Sandie in his arms, holding her loosely as he looked down at her. 'You understand that, don't you, Sandie? Nothing would be easier—or more delightful—than for me to come in now and stay the night with you. But somehow I don't think that would be right for us. Somehow, I see you in white, coming down the aisle in a drift of white. And if we'd lived together first, you wouldn't be able to do that, would you?'

Sandie's heart swelled at the vision he had created, but she looked up under her lashes and murmured: 'But the other night . . .'

He smiled. 'That wasn't meant to happen, Sandie. I'm not going to say forget it—I never will, for one— but we won't repeat it deliberately, all right? Not until—well, until you've had that white lace . . . That *is* what you want, isn't it?'

Sandie nodded. 'Yes. That's what I want.' She lifted her face for his kiss, and then opened her door. 'Good night, Sky.'

For a moment, they clung together, as desperate suddenly as if they were about to part for years. Sandie knew a brief moment of fear—suppose this were all a dream? And then Sky pushed her gently through the door and pulled it shut.

She leaned against it, dazed. He loved her—Sky actually *loved* her! All right, he had not actually said the words—but he hadn't needed to, had he? He had told her with his eyes, with his lips, with his hands. And he'd talked about their wedding. *Their* wedding—not his and Wanda's. Theirs.

Walking towards her bedroom, too bemused to do anything more than undress and slide into bed, there to lie awake and go over again every tiny detail of the magical evening she had just spent, Sandie found herself hoping that it wouldn't be too long before the wedding Sky had talked about. Because she wanted him so badly, now that he had gone, she didn't know how she was going to wait.

And she was fairly sure that he must be feeling very much the same.


'You really mean to say you think Sky Darrington is *in love* with you?' Wanda Tallon's eyes were purple with rage as she stared at the younger girl, taking in every detail of her slender figure and the check shirt and jeans she always wore around the flat. 'With *you*?'

Sandie shrugged, hoping she looked as cool as she meant to—she certainly did not feel it! 'So he says,' she returned, trying to keep her voice light. 'And I don't really see why he should say so if——'

'He's actually *said* so? In as many words?' Wanda challenged her, and to her dismay the question brought Sandie up short. He *hadn't* actually said so, she remembered—not in words. He'd found other, quite convincing, ways to tell her—but she wasn't going to tell Wanda about *that*.

'He hasn't, has he?' Wanda pursued triumphantly,

eyes gleaming. 'He's never actually *said* he loved you.' She shook her head in mock pity. 'Dear me, little Sandie, don't you ever listen to warnings? I *told* you he was just amusing himself, but did you take any notice? Not a scrap. And now you're going to get hurt. You're bound to.'

'I don't think so.' Sandie was trying desperately to cling to her certainty of Sky's love. 'I don't think Sky's amusing himself at all. He—he's talked about our wedding, he——'

'He's actually *proposed*? Set a date?'

'No, but——'

'Then it means nothing.' Wanda reached out suddenly and snatched at Sandie's left hand. 'And where's the ring? I take it you look on yourself as being engaged.'

'Yes, but . . .' Sandie had never even thought about a ring and she felt her face burn as she stared at the bare fingers. 'We—we haven't got around to it yet,' she said lamely.

'And you never will, if my guess is accurate.' Wanda watched her through slitted eyes. 'You're fooling yourself, Sandie, and if you'll take my advice you'll get yourself out of it now. Because the more seriously you take Sky Darrington and his talk of weddings, the more you're going to be hurt. *He doesn't mean a word of it*— understand?'

Sandie stared at her, conscious of the rapid beating of her heart. Why was Wanda saying these things to her? She must realise that her own talk of marriage with Sky had been seen for what it was—a pack of lies. Why was she still trying to frighten Sandie with them, still warning her off? There couldn't be any gain to her from doing so.

Unless—a thought nagged at her—there was actually some truth in what she said.

No. No. *No!*

Wanda was still watching her though those catlike eyes and Sandie remembered uncomfortably that she still didn't know a great deal about Sky. Oh, in one way she felt she knew all that there was to know—all the important things. But in other ways—well . . .

'Now, why not answer my question, the one I came here to ask?' Wanda said coaxingly. 'Just where is Sky? We were supposed to be spending the weekend together——' The information was dropped casually, like a bomb '—but he seems to have disappeared off the face of the earth. Nobody at his office knows, or will say. I came to you as a last resort. But if you say you're engaged to Sky—well, you must know, mustn't you? So why not tell me?'

'Why should I?' Sandie demanded with a return of defiance. 'Obviously, since Sky and I *are* engaged, he won't be spending the weekend with you. Or any other weekend.'

'True.' Wanda didn't seem too upset by that, Sandie noted uneasily. As if she still didn't believe it. 'I'd just like to hear it from his own lips.'

'Well, I'm afraid you won't be able to do that. I'm sure he'll have sent you some kind of message, though.' She would leave her feelings about this arrangement he'd apparently had with Wanda until later. 'Probably his secretary's trying to contact you now.'

'I doubt it. Sky and I have never communicated through a third party.' Wanda settled back in her armchair, smooth silken legs extended to show off her elegant and clearly expensive shoes. 'No, I'll wait here if you don't mind. I imagine he'll be calling in to see you.'

Sandie gazed at her, feeling totally helpless. What on earth was she to do now? Nothing but main force was going to move Wanda, that was clear. And just how long was she prepared to stay there, looking around the small and admittedly modest flat as if it were on the list for slum clearance?

'Such a sweet little place,' Wanda observed patronisingly. 'But I expect you're longing to move out, aren't you? I should imagine you'll feel rather strange at first—living in Sky's penthouse flat, and the Cotswold house. Quite different from what you've been used to.'

Sandie seethed. She could not admit that she'd never been to Sky's flat at the top of the tall office block in the Barbican. No doubt it *was* very different from this—but did Wanda *have* to be quite so dismissive? It had never looked shabby before she came in, all swathed in mink and smelling of Paris. It had always been homely and welcoming.

'Do you imagine Sky will be long?' Wanda continued, lighting a cigarette without asking permission. 'I assume he *is* coming to see you this evening.'

Pointedly, Sandie walked across the room and opened the window. 'I'm not sure,' she said, her back to Wanda, and she felt the immediate sharpening of Wanda's interest.

'Not sure? Didn't he say?' The silence hung between them. 'Do you mean he's just gone off and left you—his *fiancée*——' The word was heavy with scorn '—not knowing where he is or when he'll be back?'

'I didn't say that——' Sandie began, but to her dismay she saw that Wanda had caught up her slip like a dog snatching up a bone, and like a terrier she wasn't going to let go.

'You didn't really have to, did you? You *don't* know. He hasn't told you.' A spark of malicious pleasure showed in her purple eyes. 'You and Sky aren't quite so close as you'd like to think, are you? Now why should that be?'

Sandie bit her lip, feeling frustration wash over her.

Wanda was getting the better of her, and she shouldn't be. *Sandie* was the one who was engaged to Sky, wasn't she? So why should the older girl, glamorous and experienced though she might be, have any advantage?

She had never longed for Sky quite as much as she did then. Oh, where was he—why was he not here, standing at her side, keeping her hand warm in his as he told Wanda quite bluntly that he and Sandie were in love, were to be married, and there was never going to be any other woman in his life? Where *was* he?

Because Wanda was right, of course. Sandie *didn't* know where he was. And up till now that hadn't really bothered her. He'd rung her early that morning to tell her about the appointment he'd forgotten and to make arrangements to see her on the following Monday. He'd sounded honestly regretful—even angry with himself—and Sandie had warmed to the knowledge that he wanted to be with her, warmed to such an extent that she'd been able to overcome her own disappointment and tell him that it was quite all right and that she loved him. Even now, she was still convinced that the note of love in his voice had been genuine. There couldn't have been anything sinister in his call, in his actions. Wanda was just trying to cause trouble, but Sandie was determined not to let her.

'How close Sky and I are is our business,' she said coldly. 'We're certainly close enough for me to trust him absolutely. Even if he didn't choose to tell me where——' She stopped abruptly, but Wanda pounced at once, her face alive with glee.

'You don't know where he is, do you? You don't know when you're going to see him again—and you don't know who he's with.' Abruptly, she stood up, crushing her cigarette against a saucer. Her face was alight, gleaming with malicious triumph, and Sandie could do nothing but stare at her, a dull despair gripping her heart as she saw the delight on Wanda's face and knew that the other girl's next words were to spell disaster for her.

'Why, the aggravating man—if that isn't just like him!' Wanda said softly. 'He's gone straight down to the country—to our rendezvous—thinking that I'd be there. He's done it once before, you know—well, he has so much on his mind it's not surprising if he's a little absent-minded from time to time.' She gave Sandie a benevolent smile. 'Poor little Sandie. And you didn't know—never would have known, if I hadn't come here looking for him. Well, I expect it's a good thing in the long run. At least I've saved you from any further disillusionment.' Another charming smile. 'You will excuse me now, won't you? I'll have to fly—mustn't keep the lord and master waiting. He is apt to be a little—impatient—on these occasions, you know ...' She gathered up her glossy crocodile bag, gave herself a quick look in the mirror, then made for the door. 'Goodbye, Sandie. See you again, I expect. Um—any special message for Sky? No? Well, I expect you'll be wanting to talk with him yourself, when he gets back.' And she was gone, leaving Sandie breathless, stupefied and reeling with shock by the open window.

*Could* Wanda be right? Was Sky really, even at this moment, driving towards some pre-arranged rendezvous, some secluded little country hotel, where he would spend the weekend with Wanda, loosing all the passion he had shown just once with Sandie? It couldn't be true, it couldn't! Fiercely, she slammed the window shut and tipped the ash from the saucer into the kitchen sink, washing it away. Now the flat was as if Wanda had never been—except for a lingering remnant of cigarette smoke and a drift of French perfume. Sandie opened the window again and stared out. It *couldn't* be true . . . could it?

But Sky *had* gone away, and without telling her where, a small voice argued. And he *hadn't* actually said he loved her—or made a real proposal—or set any kind of date for the wedding. And neither had he made love to her yesterday evening, when he must have known that she was only too willing. When he must have known already that he would be going away today— and hadn't mentioned it to her.

Perhaps he hadn't made love to her because he disliked the idea of going from one woman to another, with less than twenty-four hours' interval. Was he that fastidious? That sensitive?

Half an hour ago the question wouldn't even have arisen. Now, it was with a kind of dull horror that Sandie found herself examining it with some seriousness.

No—*no!* She *couldn't* think about Sky like this— *mustn't!* He loved her, he'd made it quite clear. And she loved him. Whatever he was doing this weekend, wherever he was going, it was nothing to do with Wanda. Everything that woman had said was a lie, a poisonous lie. Told because she had lost Sky and knew it but, like the dog in the manger, didn't intend letting anyone else have him.

You know it's true, Sandie told herself harshly. You know it is.

But all the same, once the seed had been sown it was very difficult to prevent it from germinating. And as Sandie roamed aimlessly about the flat for the rest of the evening, she found herself going over and over again the brief conversation she'd had on the telephone with Sky, when he'd told her that he was sorry but he couldn't see her until the following Monday. It had

been as businesslike as that but Sandie, though
disappointed, hadn't worried about it, assuming that he
was speaking from the office and had someone with
him. But now, she began to wonder . . .

She found herself repeating in her head every word of
that conversation with Wanda; the conversation that
had left her shattered, uncertain and—she had to admit
it now—bitterly disillusioned.

## CHAPTER NINE

'WELL, that's it then,' Tim said, his boyish face breaking into the twinkling grin that was so characteristic of him. 'Everything ready for the off tomorrow. Let's hope the weather holds.'

'Mm. I've got a met. forecast.' Sandie glanced up at the sky, noting the few small puffs of cloud that were all that marred the perfect sunset. 'They seem to think it'll be OK, though there might be some wind later. What's important to us is how much later.'

'Well, the organisers have asked us to fly mid-morning and afternoon, so with any luck we'll be all right for the first flight, if not the second. Trouble is, of course, the second is when most of the crowds will be here. Oh well—we'll just have to wait and see. Can't change the weather, even to suit county show organisers.' Tim swung himself up into the driver's seat of the van. 'Coming for a meal, Sandie?'

'Yes, all right.' Sandie took a last look round the roped-off portion of the showground from which she was to fly the balloon next day. This was an important show, one of the biggest and oldest in the country, closely tied to the old autumn fairs at which cattle, sheep and geese had been marketed, and she was anxious to do well. That was why she had kept Tim here so late in the evening, checking that everything was ready for the next day. That, and because it helped to keep her mind off her troubles . . .

She had heard nothing from Sky since his 'phone call and nothing from Wanda—though she had hardly expected the older woman to contact her again. She was probably well satisfied with the damage she had done! But Sandie had hoped desperately for a call from Sky. She would have known—surely she would have known—from his voice whether or not he was deceiving her.

There had been no call, however, and she had had to resign herself to waiting until Monday. Meanwhile this show was booked and there was no excuse for her not to go ahead with it. If nothing else, it would pass the time. And so she had firmly put all her worries to the back of her mind and kept Tim and Andy checking and re-checking, until they were almost on the point of rebellion.

At last she had relented and sent Andy away—they were near enough to the Cotswolds for him to be able to go home for the night—and now she and Tim were on their way to their hotel. Sandie sighed and rested her head against the back of the seat.

'Tired?' Tim inquired, shooting her a glance. 'You've looked a bit washed out, today, if you don't mind my saying so.'

'No, I don't mind. I *feel* washed out. Probably need a break. Even ballooning can be almost like work at times!'

Tim smiled. 'Well, most of the shows are over now. Maybe you could have a holiday. You're due for one—you've been working all summer. Why don't you ask the boss?'

'Sky?' Sandie's lips quirked ruefully. She'd been expecting a honeymoon—now she wasn't sure he would even take her out to dinner again. She did not really know what she thought or expected any more. She'd thought so much about it, veering this way and that with her confused and conflicting emotions, that her mind was a turmoil and she was totally unable to pick out any clear ideas. Only by seeing Sky would she be able even to begin to sort herself out. But she wouldn't be seeing him before Monday—and in the meantime, if he were really with Wanda. . . .

'I might go away for a week or two,' she said in answer to Tim's suggestion. 'The Channel Islands perhaps. I went there in the spring, and they were beautiful, but I didn't really have time to look around.' In a sense, Guernsey was where it had all started, she thought, remembering Denis' advances and her reaction. That had led to her giving in her notice and getting the job with Sky. Maybe it would be appropriate to return there, now that it all seemed to be ending.

'Sounds fun.' Tim swung into the hotel car park and brought the van to a stop. 'Right, let's go and eat. You've kept us at it so hard today, young Sandie, I haven't had time for more than a sandwich! I now propose to make up for it. Talk about slavery and starvation!' He led the way into the hotel and through to the dining-room. 'Let's grab a menu and order ourselves a slap-up meal. Time for washing hands when we've done that.'

Rather to her surprise, Sandie found herself almost as hungry as Tim and ready to settle for a traditional roast dinner, starting with melon and finishing with apple pie. The food was good and plentiful; she realised she was enjoying it and realised too that it was the first substantial meal she had eaten since that dinner with Sky—how many days, months, years ago?

Oh God, she thought, spoon raised halfway to her lips as the thought of Sky hit her like a blow to the heart. Is it really all going to come to nothing? Was it really just a childish dream? And if so—how am I ever going to bear it? How am I going to live?

She became aware that Tim was speaking and jerked her thoughts away from Sky in time to hear him finish what was obviously a question.

'... know him?' he said inquiringly, and Sandie shook her head.

'I'm sorry, Tim. I was miles away. What did you say?'

'That man over there. He keeps looking at you—seems to know you. Do you know him?'

Sandie turned in her seat, unable at first to see the man Tim was indicating. There was a party of six, all dressed up and obviously celebrating something; a couple on their own who had eyes for no one else and were probably on their honeymoon; and—oh yes—a man, sitting alone in the corner, shadowed by a tall fern growing close by, but certainly staring in her direction. Sandie stared back, a chill goosing across her body. It couldn't be—but even as she began to turn back, the man smiled a flash of white teeth and waved. It *was*. And a tiny groan of dismay escaped her lips as he got up, with the obvious intention of coming over.

'You do know him?' Tim asked, and she nodded helplessly. There was nothing she could do about it, after all—and at least she had Tim here. For protection, she thought wryly.

'Yes, I know him. I used to work for him when I was a secretary. His name's Denis Brenchley and he's an accountant.'

'I see.' Tim looked up with ingenuous interest as Denis approached. And Sandie had to admit that her ex-boss looked impressive enough in his well-cut grey suit, with the gold watch at his wrist and the matching clips on his polished black shoes. Though she decided that she preferred Sky's understated, undecorated look, his steel watch and plain shoes. Everything about him was quality, restraint and good taste; everything about Denis was expense, flamboyance and vulgarity. Even his teeth were too white and even, she thought with distaste, and wasn't that a flash of gold there too?

'Sandie!' Denis was holding out both hands to her, but before she could decide how to respond he bent and kissed her on the cheek. 'How marvellous to see you. What are you doing around here?' His polished glance swept over Tim, assessing him immediately, Sandie could see, as little more than a callow youth. 'And is this the boyfriend?'

'No, he's my assistant. We're working here for a few days, at the county show.'

'*Are* you?' Denis looked at her with curiosity. 'And you have an assistant? What are you doing then? Tell me.'

Sandie hadn't wanted to tell him anything—she didn't want to speak to him at all and she was surprised that he wanted to speak to her—but there was no help for it. Reluctantly she said, 'We're flying a hot-air balloon. It's a crowd-puller and advertisement. We're hoping to fly twice tomorrow, weather permitting.'

'A *what*? A hot-air balloon? Did I really hear you right?' Denis gaped at them both and Sandie felt her lips twitch. 'Sandie, you're pulling my leg.'

'No, it's true,' Tim assured him earnestly. 'Sandie's a very good pilot. We've been working together for several months now.' He glanced at Sandie and she was startled to see the look of pride and affection on his face. She'd almost forgotten that Tim was still carrying a torch for her, even though he rarely showed it.

Denis had seen the look too. She caught the speculation on his face and felt a shiver of uneasiness. But Denis couldn't harm her now, even if he wanted to. And he was returning to the subject of the balloon.

'You really mean, then, that you fly balloons for a living? Sandie, I don't know whether to believe you or not. It sounds too fantastic to be true.'

'Come along tomorrow and see then,' Sandie said, and immediately regretted her words. The last person she wanted around her was Denis Brenchley. But he probably wouldn't come. He must be here on business himself—didn't the firm have some clients around the area somewhere?—and he wouldn't have time to go to county shows, especially as they definitely weren't his scene.

'Well, I suppose it must be true. Nobody would make up a story like that,' Denis shrugged, dismissing it. 'And what else have you been doing with yourself since you left us? Looking for another job, I suppose.'

'Denis, I've *got* another job—I told you, I work at ballooning now. It's what I've always wanted to do. I couldn't believe it when I got it.'

Denis looked at her and she was shocked to see a distinct hostility in his eyes. So he hadn't forgiven her for running out on him on Guernsey. Probably he'd never been rejected before. It must have been a severe blow to his ego.

'Better than being secretary to a top-flight firm of accountants, obviously,' he said coolly, and turned to Tim. 'Did Sandie ever tell you about that? Her job with us?'

Tim shook his head. 'We've never talked much about anything but ballooning,' he said with a disarming grin. 'Balloonists don't!'

But Denis was clearly unimpressed. He glanced once again from Tim to Sandie and she saw the calculation in his eyes and felt uneasy. Plainly, he hadn't believed her when she'd said Tim wasn't her boyfriend, and she wouldn't put it past him to try to stir things between them. Well, that wouldn't work—for one thing, much as she liked Tim there was never any chance of any intimate relationship between them, and she was pretty sure he knew it. For another, his devotion was too strong for any of Denis' stories to upset him. People like Tim might seen ingenuous and naïve, but they could generally see through the brash sophistication of a man like Denis Brenchley.

'Well, you must get her to tell you the whole story sometime,' Denis said now, easily. 'All about our few days on Guernsey together. It was fun, wasn't it, Sandie—while it lasted?' Again he shot her that inimitable look. 'On second thoughts, maybe it's a story that's better left untold. Let the past bury its own dead, eh, Sandie?'

'That's the most sensible thing you've said yet,' she said coolly. 'But in any case, you won't worry Tim with stories of my past—as I told you, he's my assistant and friend, and that's the way it's going to stay.'

'That right, I'm afraid,' Tim agreed with mock resignation. 'Not that I ever thought it could be any other way—not once Sky appeared on the scene.'

'Sky?' Denis queried sharply, and Sandie gave a silent groan.

'Our boss,' Tim supplied. 'Sky Darrington—head of Standish, Darrington and Bryce, the advertising agency. That's who we work for. Sky's set up a balloon stable, carrying advertisements for various firms and sponsors, and we fly one of the balloons. Or at least Sandie does.'

'And this Sky Darrington—he and Sandie are——' Denis left the sentence unfinished. but his eyes were sharp, darting from one to the other. Sandie stared down at her plate, feeling the flush rise steadily up her neck and over her cheeks. What on earth was Tim going to say next?

'Oh gosh, I'm not saying that,' Tim said hurriedly. 'Look, I shouldn't have said that much—I'm sorry, Sandie, I never meant—It's just that Sky's the kind of man—well, you know . . .' He floundered to a halt, confused and embarrassed, looking so wretchedly apologetic that Sandie felt compelled to reassure him, though she could cheerfully have hit him over the head with the empty wine-bottle. Denis, however, had clearly gained enormous delight from Tim's tactless utterances. He looked as smugly satisfied as a cat as he rose to leave them.

'I know just what you mean,' he told Tim, laying a friendly hand on the younger man's shoulder for a moment. His eyes as he looked across at Sandie had lost their hostility, warming almost to friendliness—the friendliness of an enemy who sees victory in his grasp, she thought miserably. 'Well, it's been good to see you again, Sandie. We must keep in touch. I'll give you a ring, all right?'

'If you like,' she said, determining never to speak to him again if she could possibly help it. 'But I move about quite a bit now, you know. I rather doubt if we'll bump into each other again.' And I certainly hope not, she added with her eyes. But Denis' complacent expression never faltered. He nodded goodnight and left them walking out of the dining-room with the easy assurance of a man who is used to all the best places.

'Sandie, I'm sorry,' Tim said as soon as he had gone. 'I never meant to say all that. I don't know what got into me—the wine, I guess. Better stick to lemonade from now on.'

'Oh, it's all right,' Sandie folded her napkin. 'I don't expect to see him again anyway, so whatever you said wouldn't make any difference. I just——' She hesitated for a moment. 'Tim, I'd just like to know what people are saying about me and Sky—if they're saying anything, that is.'

'Well, nothing really. I mean, nobody's *talking* about you, don't think that.' Tim was still obviously embarrassed and would like to have said no more, but Sandie's fixed look kept him going. 'It's only that Sky's changed lately—changed in his attitudes. I mean, I've always liked him and looked up to him—but he could be odd at times, sort of distant. And for a while now he hasn't been—except just lately again, since the Wales flight. He seems more—well, human, I suppose you'd call it. And we all reckoned it was because of you. You make him different.' He paused. 'And about women—well, he's never had any trouble with getting girlfriends, but they've always been like Wanda, all glossy and fashion-plate, you know what I mean. And yet he's never seemed to actually *like* them very much. But you—you're different. You're real. I've seen him looking at you—as if he couldn't believe his eyes at first, and then—well, as if you warmed him. Like a fire on a cold day.' Tim stopped, even more embarrassed, then muttered, 'If you ask me, I'd say he was crazy about you. And I wouldn't blame him, either.'

There was a long silence. Tim's eyes were fixed on the table now and Sandie watched him without speaking, conscious that those last words hadn't been easy to say. Then she stretched out her hand and covered his.

'Thank you, Tim,' she said softly. 'That was very nice of you. I just wish—well, to be quite honest, I wish you were right. In fact, for a while I did think—but no. Sky doesn't really want me, Tim. I know that now. Oh yes, maybe you were right in saying that I was different—but it's the Wanda kind of girl he really likes. The kind who can take love and leave it without a backward glance. He doesn't want to get involved with someone like me, who doesn't understand that attitude.'

'Then he's a fool,' Tim said abruptly, and his unwontedly serious face broke into its familiar grin. 'And I never thought I'd be saying *that* about Sky Darrington! See what an effect you've had on *me*, Sandie!'

'And on that note, I think we'll say goodnight.' Sandie stood up and held out a hand to Tim. 'Thanks for being so patient with me, Tim. I know I've been extra-fussy today. It just seemed to help, somehow. I promise I'll be back to normal tomorrow.'

They went up the stairs together and said goodnight. Tim's room was several doors away from Sandie's; he gave her a cheerful little wave and went towards it. Sandie watched him fondly. He was a good friend, Tim. If only she could have fallen in love with him!

But life wasn't like that, was it? she mused as she sat down on her bed and stared blankly at the opposite wall. Life made you fall in love with the wrong people—people who played on your emotions as on a musical instrument, then dropped you when the tune no longer pleased them and left you without melody in your life. Left you flat; left you despairing . . .

The shrill ring of the telephone jerked her out of her depression. For a moment, she stared at the instrument, heart beating wildly. Who knew she was here? Only Sky—and the ground crew. Tim had only just said goodnight and she couldn't believe that Andy or the others would be telephoning her. So could it possibly be . . .?

She grabbed the receiver, suddenly afraid that it would stop, that her caller might change his mind. 'Yes?' she said, breathless as if she'd run a race. 'Sandie Lewis here. Is that—is that——'

'Denis Brenchley,' the smooth voice said, and her heart sank like a stone. 'Thought we could have another

little chat, without the boy this time. Unless he's still
with you . . .?'

'No, he's not,' she snapped, disappointment churning
her stomach. 'And I don't think there's anything we
have to talk about, Denis——'

'Oh, I don't agree there,' the smooth tones
contradicted. 'I think we have a great deal to talk
about. Like where you went that night on Guernsey,
when you ran off so impulsively. Did you realise you
never even said goodnight to me? Nor goodbye when
you took it into your head to leave the next day? It
put me in quite an embarrassing position, Sandie. Not
only then, when I had to explain to Geoffrey where
and why you'd suddenly departed—told him some
story about a sick relative, if I remember rightly—but
when I got back to London too and found you'd
handed in your notice and gone. Yes, a very
embarrassing position. And I don't like being embarrassed. Sandie.'

'That's a pity,' she said, his long speech having given
her time to recover herself a little. 'Perhaps in future
you won't force people to embarrass you in that way.'

'In future?' he said musingly. 'Now, that's just what I
want to talk about, Sandie. The future. Yours and
mine.'

'*Our* future?' she repeated unbelievingly. 'We don't
have one! We never did.'

'And that's just what I'm not quite so sure about.
That's just what I'd like to discuss with you, Sandie.
Sometime soon. Now, for instance.'

'You're out of your mind,' Sandie said coldly.
'There's nothing to discuss. And if you don't mind, I'm
tired and I want to go bed—alone.'

'Tomorrow, then,' he persisted. 'You're free in the
evening, aren't you? Staying here again? Get rid of the

little boy, Sandie, and come out to dinner with me. I've got things to say to you.'

'Nothing I'm interested in,' Sandie moved to put down the 'phone, but just caught his next words and lifted it again. '*What* did you say?'

'I said, if you won't let me say them to you maybe I should talk to that boss of yours. Sky Darrington. The one who has all the women at his feet. I imagine that was what your young friend was implying. All the women, —including Sandie Lewis, the untouchable, last of the quaint old-fashioned virgins. If you still are.' He paused. 'Now any man who can achieve *that* is a man I'd very much like to meet.'

Sandie was silent. Her heart was thumping so much she felt sick—or was it Denis' insinuations that were making her feel nauseated? 'Just what are you getting at, Denis?' she asked at last.

'Meet me for dinner and find out,' he said silkily, and she knew that she would have to. 'Eight tomorrow evening, Sandie, all right? We won't eat here—we'll go out to a nice little place I know in the country. And then—well, we'll see, won't we?'

Sandie put down her receiver, feeling sick at heart. There was nothing she wanted to do less than have dinner with Denis—particularly at some 'nice little place in the country'. Suppose he took her out to some remote spot and then made a pass at her? Would he have the nerve? She knew already that she couldn't fight him, that struggling only excited him further. Could she risk it?

And could she *not*? Could she ignore his demands, knowing that if she did so he would almost certainly go to Sky and tell him about that night on Guernsey— making it seem as if she'd gone willingly to share a suite with him in the hotel, making it appear that she'd stayed all night? Because she had no proof that she didn't, she remembered miserably. Nobody had seen her leave the hotel that night, or return to it next morning. As far as the management was concerned, she'd been there all the time.

If she did call Denis' bluff, would he go to Sky with his story? Would Sky believe him? And—the thought hit her like a punch—would it even matter? For Sky was away with Wanda, wasn't he—and whether he would want Sandie again when he returned was anybody's guess.

Anyone with an ounce of gumption, she told herself fiercely, would tell Sky Darrington just where to go. But she wasn't at all sure that she would do that. Whatever he did, she still loved him, deeply and whole-heartedly. And the thought of him believing in Denis' story brought an ever heavier misery to her throbbing mind.

She would have to go with Denis tomorrow evening. What happened then lay largely in the lap of the gods. It couldn't make things much worse, anyway.

Or so she believed.

Sandie had half a mind the next evening to meet Denis in the same red tracksuit that she had been wearing all day for flying. Perhaps then he would think again about taking her out to dinner—Denis had always liked well-groomed women, she remembered. But her own pride wouldn't allow her to appear in front of him looking anything less than her best. She wanted Denis to know that she could still be feminine in spite of doing what he might consider a man's job. Accordingly, she washed her hair and brushed it until it shone like palest spun gold, then dressed in a new suit with jade green paisley skirt, matching waistcoat and toning green blouse with a tie neck. The strong colour set off her hair and deepened the green of her eyes, which she made up carefully so that the whole effect was striking enough to turn even Sky Darrington's head.

Sky. She paused, the eyeliner still in her hand. This suit had been bought with him in mind. She had intended wearing it—her mind shied away from the thought, but she had intended wearing it on the day he gave her his ring. Now it seemed impossible that she could ever really have believed he would give her an engagement ring, a wedding ring or a ring of any kind. Sadness washed over her, then an angry determination. All right, so Sky had been two-timing her. Leading her on, for whatever foul purposes of his own. Well, she was not going to sit in her room and brood over it any more. She had done enough of that. She was going to go out and *enjoy* herself.

Even if it was with Denis. And even if Denis intended her no good at all.

With head high and defiantly glittering eyes, Sandie went down to the foyer. She saw Denis turn to look at her as she came down the curving staircase, and was well pleased with his reaction—the widening of his eyes, the appraising look that followed—both were eminently satisfactory. All right, my boy, so you're still smarting over Guernsey, she thought—well, maybe by the end of this evening you'll have decided to forget that. Not that it matters. You're still not going to get what you want. And whatever you tell Sky isn't going to make an atom of difference between us. Whatever I thought we had, it's over. Finished. So tonight—just for once—little Sandie Lewis is in charge. Tonight, I'm going to enjoy myself—and to hell with *all* the male sex. They've played around with me and my emotions quite long enough. Now, it's *my* turn.

'Hello, Denis,' she smiled, coming up close and smiling into his eyes. 'I hope I haven't kept you waiting.'

'If you had, I might well consider the wait worthwhile,' he returned, still appraising her with his eyes. 'Well, well, Sandie—you've really pushed the boat out tonight, haven't you—you look stunning. Am I to take it that you've reconsidered your attitude?'

'Reconsidered it?' Sandie said innocently, head on one side. 'I don't know what you mean, Denis.'

'Oh no?' His look could only be described as old-fashioned. 'Last night you couldn't wait to see the back of me, and I didn't get the impression you were too enthusiastic over the 'phone. Yet now you arrive all smiles, dressed to kill—so what gives, Sandie? Not that I don't approve of the change.'

Sandie shrugged delicately. 'Oh, well, it seemed silly to go on being at loggerheads, just because of a—misunderstanding—six months ago. We always got on well, didn't we Denis? I just thought it was time to forget the past. Start again.' She glanced up under her lashes, amazed by her own performance. Coquetry had never been part of her repertoire. Wanda would be proud of me, she thought with a tiny giggle, and wondered if she was overdoing it. Surely even Denis wouldn't be taken in by this act.

But it seemed that he was. His ego was expanding visibly as he slipped his arm around her waist and steered her out of the hotel entrance to his car. He'd got a new model, she noticed, a sleek silver-grey with an aggressive look to it that said a lot about its owner. Inside, it was all plushy comfort and she suspected that the seats would recline right back. It was that sort of car, and Denis was that sort of motorist.

'I've booked a table at the *Iron Duke*,' he told her as

he wove through the evening traffic. 'Used to be called the *Wellington* but they gave it the boot.' Sandie laughed dutifully. 'You'll like it there. Quiet, intimate, and good food. How did the ballooning go?'

'Very well. Daytime flying's a bit risky sometimes, you can get tricky winds and thermals, but today it was almost ideal. I think the show organisers were pleased, and the sponsors will be too. We attracted a lot of interest and there was a view of the balloon in one of the shots on the local TV news.' She stopped. Denis was clearly not really interested, although he had his 'listening' face on—the one she had seen when he was dealing with clients who bored him. A quick flash of anger scorched through her, and she determined to make him listen. But Denis was like Sky, wasn't he?—a man saw women as useful for only one thing. The only time either was prepared to give a woman his full attention was when in bed—and that just wasn't enough.

'Tell me what you've been doing since I left,' she suggested, as if it were the one thing that had been occupying her mind for the past five months. 'I've often thought about you——' *that* was true! '——and wondered how you were getting along. What happened about the Stuart trust?'

Never one to miss an opportunity to talk about himself, Denis launched forth into a detailed account of his doings since Sandie had left the firm. From what he said, she found it difficult to understand why he had not been made a full partner, and said so, hoping that he wouldn't see that her tongue was firmly in her cheek. Denis, however, took her remark perfectly seriously and agreed that it was odd.

'Shouldn't be too long now, though,' he said confidently. 'Old Terrance will be retiring soon and I

can't see who else could step into his shoes. Peter
Wright certainly couldn't.' He went on to extol his own
virtues and decry those of the other members of the
firm, while Sandie kept a tight check on her boredom
and impatience with his conceit, listened attentively and
made—she hoped—all the right replies.

The *Iron Duke* was about ten miles out of town—ten
miles of countryside, some of it woodland, Sandie
noticed, thinking somewhat nervously of the journey
back. It was all very well to lead Denis along, but could
she really handle him? She'd only managed to get away
in Guernsey by luck, and he wasn't likely to give her
such a chance again . . . She shrugged. Why worry?
Leave it to take care of itself. Denis might think he was
God's gift to womankind, but she didn't think he would
actually *rape* her.

All the same, she was beginning to wish she hadn't
given him quite so much encouragement as they entered
the inn, Denis with his arm once more familiarly
around her waist, his fingers straying a little further
than she liked. Still, it didn't really matter. The lighting
was dim in the ancient bar with its dark timbers and
inglenook. And there was nobody here that she knew.

In a mood of recklessness, she allowed Denis to lead
her to the darkest corner and seat her on a small,
chintz-covered settee just big enough for two. She made
no demur when he settled himself beside her, just too
close for comfort, and didn't refuse the large and potent
cocktail he ordered. She forced herself not to shrink
away when he slipped his arm around her shoulders and
drew her against him so that her head rested on his
shoulder.

It was only much later that she realised that her
behaviour was as much a retaliation against Sky's
treatment of her as against Denis'. Only much later that

she knew that she had asked for everything that was to happen to her that night. At the time, she did not stop to analyse her actions. She only knew that there wasn't a man in the world she wouldn't have treated in exactly the same way. They're all the same, she thought with a savage misery as she lifted her glass and smiled into Denis' eyes. All out for what they can get. And it was up to women to see that they got what they deserved. All women—and all men.

She tilted her head to one side, flirted her lashes and teased Denis along, knowing all the time that she intended to let him down and enjoying the thought. There was a strange, febrile excitement in what she was doing and it lent a feverish sparkle to her over-bright green eyes, a hectic flush to her cheeks. What did it matter what happened to her this evening? Sky didn't love her after all. He was away somewhere with Wanda. And beside that fact, nothing mattered.

But in that, she was wrong. As she discovered the moment she followed Denis into the dining-room—and saw Sky, sitting alone at a corner table, his corn-gold hair as bright as a lamp and his eyes burning like twin blue flames as he stared straight across the room and saw her.

The sight brought her up short, hand to her throat, heart kicking like a frightened deer. Suddenly panic-stricken, she tried to disengage herself from Denis' possessive grasp. But Denis, thinking that she was teasing him, merely chuckled and gripped her a little more tightly and familiarly.

Sandie watched in helpless dismay as Sky's eyes widened. For a long moment their glances met, locked. She saw his astonishment change to disbelief and then, as he took in her intimate closeness to Denis, a bleak and bitter contempt. Deliberately, he let his eyes rake her body, taking in every detail of her dress, her overdone make-up, her bright and too-excited eyes, her flushed face. Then he turned away again, presenting his back to them both as Denis ushered Sandie into her seat. And she knew with a cold despair exactly what she had been doing; knew that it would do no good; knew that she loved Sky even now, and always would.

And knew that her appearance with Denis had finished for ever any chance of repairing her relationship with him. From the way Sky stood up and walked out of the dining-room, it didn't seem as if he meant to give her the chance to explain. Not that there was any explanation she could give.

She had blown it this time—blown it for good.

# CHAPTER TEN

SANDIE'S ebullient and defiant mood had evaporated from the moment she met Sky's contemptuous glance across the dimly-lit dining-room. She was aware of Denis' bewilderment and growing anger as she struggled listlessly through the delicious food he ordered for her; she knew that her previous ploy, of coaxing him along only to let him down, would have worked, though it might have done her little good; just given her some temporary satisfaction in her sudden vendetta against the male sex. But now, as she made no secret of the fact that he held no attraction for her whatsoever, she could sense his returning hostility and knew that it boded ill. Denis would remember now that he had threatened to tell Sky about what had happened on Guernsey—or rather, his version, what *hadn't* happened. And if she didn't flatter his ego, make him feel good again, he would do just that.

Well, she thought dully, he might as well. Sky had seen them together now, seen Denis with his arm around her, seen her accepting his familiarity without protest. He had drawn his own conclusions and they had been enough to send him out of the room without acknowledging her. It didn't really matter what Denis told him. Nothing was going to make any difference now.

'If you don't want a dessert, we may as well be going,' Denis said then, breaking into the silence that had fallen between them. 'As I said, I have things to say to you, Sandie—and this isn't really the place.' He let his eyes move slowly over her. 'I'd just like to know what happened to change you this evening—you were all smiles earlier on and then you just clammed up. What happened? Something I said?'

He might as well know, she thought wearily. 'No. Nothing you said. Just that Sky Darrington—my boss—was in here when we arrived and saw us together. That's all.'

'That's all? Seems to be quite a lot, as far as you're concerned.' Denis looked at her, eyes narrowing. 'That boy—Tim—he implied there was something between you, and you denied it. But it's true, isn't it? There *is* something. The question is, just what.' He eyed her reflectively. 'He didn't come and speak to you—didn't ask what the hell you were doing here with another man. So you're not *that* close. But you'd like to be, wouldn't you. Maybe there's been a row, is that it? And you were hoping to make it up—and now you don't think there's a chance. Not now he's seen you with me.' The eyes took a glitter of satisfaction. 'Well, well, little Sandie, the untouchable, the virgin—all in pieces over a man. Who'd have thought to see the day?' He glanced at the bill and dropped some notes on the plate. 'This gives quite a new dimension to the whole thing. Maybe Sky's back at the hotel now, watching the clock, waiting for you to come home. Maybe I could have a word with him then—about Guernsey. But first—well, we'll see.' He drew out her chair and ushered her from the dining-room. 'This could be very interesting—as well as a lot of fun.'

'Denis——' Sandie was growing more and more alarmed. Denis' remarks were cryptic, but not too cryptic—she could guess at the meaning behind them. And she knew that to go with him now in that sleek and shiny car with its reclining seats would be to ask for trouble. Yet what else could she do? She was at least ten miles out of town, on a quiet road—she couldn't risk hitch-hiking, even if she had been able to get away from him. Bitterly now, she regretted her teasing behaviour of the earlier part of the evening. She had roused Denis quite deliberately, then withdrawn herself. It was no wonder that his eyes now had that excited, malicious gleam in them. She had been asking for trouble ever since she had decided to wear her new suit and make up her face. And now he knew about Sky too—well, whatever she got now would be no more than she deserved.

'Denis,' she began again, desperately, 'I'm sorry—I didn't mean to——' She floundered, hot with confusion under that cynical gaze. 'Please, just take me back to the hotel,' she said in a low voice. 'I've got rather a headache.'

'But of course,' he said with mock reassurance. 'Whatever else did you think I intended to do?' And he led her out to the car as if she were fragile porcelain, helping her in and fastening her seat-belt as if he were the epitome of gallant chivalry.

Well, maybe he *would* just take her back, she thought hopefully. Maybe even Denis tired of games after a while. Maybe he'd had such a boring evening that he would be glad to deposit her and never see her again.

Maybe.

It seemed at first that she was right. Denis drove away from the restaurant without speaking, without even looking at her, his profile cool in the moonlight. He seemed almost to have forgotten she was there, and she began to breathe a little more easily. She had got away with it, she thought in relief. She did not deserve to, but she'd actually got away with it.

Relaxing a little, she glanced out of the window. This

part of the country was new to her and they were driving now through thick woods. Funny—she didn't remember them on the way here. Was Denis going back by a different route? Sandie sat up and looked more attentively at the dark mass of trees. They *hadn't* come this way, she was sure. So what . . . why . . .?

'Denis,' she began, a tiny edge of panic in her voice, and then stopped as he swung the car in under the trees and came to a halt. 'Denis——' The panic was sharp now '—what are you doing? Why have you stopped here?'

'Come now, Sandie,' he murmured, and to her dismay he moved closer to her and slid one arm around her shoulders, 'don't tell me you weren't expecting this. . . .'

'I—no, I didn't want—I never meant——'

'But you did.' His voice was hard now. 'You most certainly did. Don't try to fool me, Sandie. You intended this all along—right from the start when you came down those stairs looking like some film starlet out to get a part by any means possible—including the producer's couch. You never meant it to come to anything, I know you well enough to realise that—but you meant to make me want you. If only for the pleasure of letting me down at the end. Isn't that the truth? *Isn't it?*'

His hand was under her chin now, forcing her to look at him. Her heart sank as she realised that Denis had known all along what she was doing, and probably why, though she hardly knew that herself. The mood of gay defiance she had started the evening with had dissolved completely, leaving her confused about her own motives. All she knew was that whatever she had set out to do had worked only too well; that here she was, alone with Denis in a lonely wood; that he intended to exact from her every ounce of payment he believed she owed him for that humiliation on Guernsey—and that there was absolutely nothing she could do about it.

And that Sky had seen them together, would probably see her eventual return to the hotel, and would then never want to see her again.

'Denis——' Her pleas would have little effect, she knew, but she had to make them all the same. 'Don't, I beg you—I'm sorry about this evening, I've behaved badly I know, but——'

'Not half as badly as you're going to behave,' he murmured, his hands moving over her body in a way that had her shuddering with fear and revulsion. 'Don't worry, little Sandie—I'm not going to do anything you don't like. Believe me—I'm going to *make* you like it. You're going to be begging me for it before I've finished with you.' He laid his lips on her mouth and she gasped and tried frantically to twist her head aside. 'Struggle all you want, little untouchable,' he whispered, his breath hot in her ear. 'It makes it all the better as far as I'm concerned. And don't pretend you're not enjoying it too ... you don't fool me. Not any more . . .'

Panic struck her heart like a blow and she abandoned all restraint, struggling in his arms like a trapped rabbit, lashing out with fists and arms and legs, using her knees as weapons as well as teeth and nails in this wild fight for survival. She heard Denis give a low, exultant chuckle and fought even harder, a grunt of pain spurring her on until she felt his grip relax and was able to scrabble for the door-handle. She had just found it when Denis recovered and grabbed at her wrist, jerking it away from the door—but in doing so he enabled her to open it, and Sandie felt herself falling backward,

Denis on top of her. They hit the ground with a bump, a wild tangle of arms and legs, and she heard that terrifying triumphant laugh again as Denis found her mouth with his own and let his hands roam once more over her defenceless body. His own weight was enough now to render her totally helpless, and she felt herself go limp with despair, certain now that nothing could prevent the inevitable end to this horrifying encounter.

And then, miraculously, she heard footsteps and Sky's voice, harsh and furious, from somewhere above their heads. Somehow she dragged her face away from Denis' marauding lips, her eyes searching the darkness and finding against the moon a bulky shadow that could only be Sky Darrington. A sob of relief escaped her throat as she saw the shadow loom nearer and felt Denis' weight lifted bodily away from her. Shakily, she sat up and watched as the two figures mingled, merged and then separated with a thud of flesh on bone. Denis staggered, grunted, and fell; then scrambled unsteadily to his feet.

'What the hell——?' he muttered, rubbing a hand across his chin. 'Who in God's name are you? What's the idea? If you're thinking of robbing me——'

'Only of one thing,' Sky said crisply. 'And that happens to belong to *me*—not you. And don't try to come back at me, Brenchley—I've eaten bigger things than you for breakfast. Just get out of here, and think yourself lucky to get away so lightly.'

'Now look here,' Denis blustered, 'I don't know who you think you are, but you've no right to come here busting up a perfectly innocent—innocent party. Maybe you got the wrong idea, but this is my girlfriend and everything's fine—OK, we like things a bit wild but that's nothing to do with you. So maybe *you're* the one who should get out.'

'I don't think so.' Sky was rubbing his knuckles reflectively. 'And I'm not prepared to argue about it. But we'll give the lady the last word, shall we?' He glanced down at Sandie but his head, silhouetted against the moonlit sky, was too dark for her to read his expression. 'What about it, Sandie? Do you want to go back to the hotel, or do you want to stay here? And whichever you decide—is it to be with him or with me?'

Out of the corner of her eye, Sandie saw Denis gaping at them both, but she couldn't spare any thoughts for him now. She looked up at Sky, knowing that even now things were far from being settled. There would be a lot of explaining to do, on both sides. But there was never any doubt as to her answer. She hadn't expected ever to get the chance to explain, and already her heart was beginning to sing.

'I'll go with you, Sky, please,' she said shakily and found time then to enjoy Denis' reaction as he turned to stare down at her.

*'Sky?* This is *Sky Darrington?* Your boss—the man——' Denis shook his head slowly, then said with a sudden anger: 'Is this all some kind of conspiracy? A put-up job? Because if it is——'

'No, it's not that.' Sandie scrambled to her feet and moved close to Sky's side. 'I'm sorry, Denis. I did behave badly towards you tonight—but no more badly than you've behaved to me. Let's consider ourselves equal, shall we? And leave it at that. There was never anything for you with me, you know.'

'You're telling me,' he muttered ungraciously, then shrugged. 'Well, that seems to be that. I guess I'd better be going.' He turned away, towards his car, and slammed the passenger door. 'I just hope you know what you're taking on, Darrington,' he added over his shoulder. 'That girl's a real little spitfire. Oh, she may *look* as if butter wouldn't melt in her mouth—but you just try her with half a pound. I reckon you've got yourself a right little handful there.'

'I reckon so too,' Sky agreed, and his arm came round Sandie's waist to hold her hard against him. 'In fact, I've always reckoned so.' They watched as Denis got into his car and drove away with a roar. 'And this time,' Sky went on, turning Sandie towards him, 'I don't intend to let go.' He bent his head and touched her lips with his own; and the familiar fire, the searing, scorching flame of desire, leapt between them.

Sandie gave one little groan of pure relief. Without any volition, her arms went round Sky, holding him close against her melting body. Everything that had gone before was forgotten—his inexplicable behaviour over the balloon flight, his apparent coolness before he had come at last to her flat; his ambiguous proposal, his weekend with Wanda, his unexpected appearance in the restaurant tonight. Nothing mattered but this—that they were together again, close in each other's arms, lips and bodies and hearts meeting in a wild, joyous ecstasy of reunion.

Reason fled as they each gave way to a frenzy of desire, the white heat of their passion searing their veins, driving their tormented bodies to a mad search for fulfilment. Sky's hands were almost cruel as he gripped Sandie closer, the power of his caresses lifting her into a realm she hadn't known existed. On their previous encounter, there had been an element of restraint, of exploration, introduction. Now their bodies came together as if they were two halves of a whole that had been sundered for too long; and when Sky lowered Sandie to the soft bed of newly-fallen leaves at their feet and, with a torn cry as if he could wait no longer, gave

that final thrust which brought them together, the crash
was almost audible. And Sandie, giving one last wild
glance at the branch-etched night above, felt her body
respond with such a violent convulsive wrench that for
a moment she feared it might tear her apart.

Afterwards, they lay entwined together on their bed
of leaves. Sandie ran her hand down Sky's body,
marvelling at the boneless feel of limbs and torso that
only moments before had been like iron, hard about
her. She moved closer, wanting to feel the warmth of
his skin against hers, and felt his lips in her hair. Desire
warmed her again as she turned her face up to his, but
she knew it was too soon yet. Perhaps later ... in a
little while ... She sighed; a sigh of pure, deep
contentment.

'And now,' Sky murmured in her ear, 'don't you
think a few explanations are due?'

'From you, or from me?' she whispered back
provocatively. 'Or maybe we'd better leave them unsaid
and start afresh.'

He was silent for a few moments. 'No. I don't think
so. There was obviously some good reason why you
were out with Brenchley tonight, and if I don't know it
I shall always wonder. Just as you must wonder
about—well, whatever it was that caused you to do it.
Just why was it, Sandie? You clearly didn't like the
man, yet you came into that restaurant as if you had
eyes for no one else. I can't help saying it was a nasty
shock.'

'Yes,' she said soberly. 'I'm sorry about that, Sky. I
didn't know you were going to be there.' She bit back
her question about that—Sky deserved to have his
answer first. 'Sky, I've been in such a muddle. I didn't
know where you were—or why you'd gone away. I—I
thought you didn't want me any more.' Her voice broke

and she hid her face against his shoulder, realising only now the horror of such a situation.

'Didn't *want* you? What on earth gave you that idea?'

She moved her shoulders. 'It was Wanda. She came to the flat, looking for you. She—she said you had a date. For a weekend together. She told me you were just amusing yourself with me, that it meant nothing to you and that you and she were getting married. She said you must have gone on to wherever you were supposed to be meeting, and she was going to join you there.' Sandie wriggled free of his arms and leaned up on one elbow. 'Sky, I didn't know what to believe. It all sounded so—so likely. I'd seen you together—seen the way she kissed you, hung on to you. I couldn't believe that you could really want me while Wanda was available.'

'Couldn't you? And why not?' His voice was grim.

'Well, because—because of the sort of person I am and the sort of woman Wanda is. And because of what you said—about me not enjoying being a woman. You didn't think I was feminine enough—but Wanda certainly is, and you'd always preferred that sort of woman. It seemed quite likely that you'd just—just amused yourself with me up in Radnor. I could believe that—and believe that you had a date for the weekend with her. I mean, what man *would* look at me, with Wanda around?'

'Quite a few, I should think,' he said curtly. 'Including me. Sandie, Sandie, when are you going to stop thinking of yourself as a nobody? You never used to. You came to me that day in the Barbican full of fire and spirit, and I admired you for it. You've always stood up to me, fighting like a little bantam, and I've never seen your green eyes spark without wanting to kiss you. Yet one word from that bitch Wanda, and you buckle up and lose all confidence. Why?'

'I don't know,' Sandie muttered, hardly able to believe she'd heard right. 'Perhaps because of you; because you so obviously admire her——'

'But I *don't!*' Sky reached up and shook her, then drew her down in his arms again, holding her tightly against him. 'Sandie, I don't admire her at all. I don't love her. I don't *like* her, dammit. Look, I've been all sorts of a fool. It's no wonder you've been confused. I haven't been exactly clear in my own mind.' He rolled her off him, laying her on her back and leaning up over her, his face serious in the moonlight. 'All right, I've always gone for women like Wanda—hard, polished, experienced women. But not because I *like* them—I don't. Because I'm a man who needs women—physically. And until now, I've been afraid of the emotional side of a relationship with a woman. I've been afraid of falling in love.' He paused. 'That's why I've avoided women like you, Sandie,' he said softly. 'I've always known, deep down, that your kind of girl is the kind I really need. I've always known that I could only find a deep involvement, a complete commitment, with a girl like you. A real woman. Flesh and blood rather than polish and sophistication. And that's something I've always been rather scared of—that complete commitment. So I've avoided your sort of girl and restricted myself to the women who wanted what I wanted myself—or thought I did. A good time with no strings.' He stopped again, and this time the pause was longer before he went on, his voice so low she could barely hear it. 'And then, one spring day, you blew into my office like a breath of fresh air. There was nothing I could do about it. From the moment I saw you, I was committed—however hard I tried to fight it.'

'And did you?' Sandie whispered. 'Fight it?'

'God, yes!' He gave a short laugh. 'I fought like hell.

Brought Wanda on to the scene—quarrelled with you on every conceivable occasion—tried my damnedest to resist you. Only I couldn't. I couldn't resist your sweet body, your inviting lips.' He drew her close again, his mouth trailing fire over her face and neck. 'I can't resist you now,' he muttered thickly. 'Oh God, Sandie ... Sandie ...'

This time the frenzy was less, but the sweetness and fulfilment were, if anything, increased. Sandie lay in Sky's arms, her body pulsating with his, the rhythmic melody of love beating her heart like a drum, and she didn't want it ever to end. This was what life was for—this glorious, rapturous union between man and woman. This was what it was all about—the growing, the striving, the searching. And when found, it was too precious ever to let go, and she held Sky with a sudden desperation, praying that nothing would part them again.

'So just what were you doing in that restaurant with Brenchley?' Sky asked, when they were at last able to speak again. 'Had you given me up after what Wanda had told you? Or was there something more?'

Briefly, Sandie told him about Denis—the episode on Guernsey, his appearance in the hotel the night before, the threats he had made. Briefly, she told him about her own mood of despairing defiance, her sudden urge to revenge herself on the male sex. 'But it didn't last,' she concluded ruefully. 'The moment I saw you in that restaurant I knew I'd made a dreadful mistake. I knew that I loved you and would go on loving you, whatever happened. When you looked at me with such contempt and then got up and walked out, I could have killed myself.'

'I could have killed you too,' he said soberly. 'And Brenchley. I went through hell for the next couple of

hours, while you were still in there. I waited in the other
bar to see what you would do, where you would go.
And when you came out—well, I had to follow you. I
had to know.' She felt a shudder run through his body.
'I nearly went mad when he pulled in under these trees.
And I was still in a mood for murder when I realised
that you weren't so willing after all—once I knew that,
everything was all right again. Except that I had to
restrain myself from hitting Brenchley as hard as I
wanted to!'

'But why *were* you in that restaurant?' Sandie asked,
wriggling into a more comfortable position in his arms
and watching the moon sail above. 'Just where had you
been, Sky?'

'On a perfectly innocent business trip, just as I told
you.' He gave her a tiny kiss. 'Wanda was suffering
from pique because I'd told her it was the end for us—
and she also knew about my trip, so decided to throw in
her little spanner and upset you, knowing that you
wouldn't be able to contact me to find out the truth.
But what she didn't know was that I was also going to
contact a jeweller friend of mine about an engagement
ring. We'd arranged to meet in that restaurant and in
fact he'd left only just before you arrived. I was going
to come straight to the hotel and give it to you.' He sat
up and felt in his pocket. 'I'll give it to you now,
Sandie,' he said softly. 'A little late in the day,
perhaps—and I warn you, our engagement is going to
be a short one. The ring I want to put on your finger is
the plain gold one that will bind you to me for life. This
is just a temporary arrangement, all right?'

The moonlight shone down on the diamond that he
slipped on to Sandie's finger, and she gave a tiny gasp
of delight as a glow of fire lit her slim hand. An
engagement ring—he'd gone there to collect an

engagement ring, and then seen his fiancée come in with another man. No wonder there'd been contempt in his eyes and murder in his heart. She turned to him, wanting to unburden her guilt, and knew that there was no need. All that had gone before was wiped out, forgiven and forgotten in this magical moment. From now on, they were beginning anew.

'I love you, Sky Darrington,' she said simply, and he gathered her once again close against his heart.

'I love you too, Sandie Lewis,' he said, and with those words gave her his final commitment.

It was a fine October day when they got married. The trees were tawny flames of red and gold and deep, burnished brown against the still blue sky. The air smelled very faintly of smoke from garden bonfires, and the shimmering dew of early morning had given way to a crisp freshness. Around the garden of Sky's Cotswold house, where the reception was being held, there were shaggy chrysanthemums where Sandie had once seen daffodils, a rainbow of dahlias where tulips had marched.

Sandie moved among the crowd, dazed with happiness. She hadn't realised that she and Sky had so many friends—including her own family and his, there must have been a hundred people thronging the gracious rooms, all of them apparently delighted with the match and all wanting to talk to them. Until she began to wonder if they would ever be allowed to leave on honeymoon—the honeymoon that Sky had insisted on keeping a secret from her as well as from everyone else.

Or—perhaps not quite everyone else. Tim and Andy kept looking at her with twitching lips, as if they knew something. And her cousin Con, home from Africa specially for the occasion, also seemed to be in on it. But nothing she could say would induce them to tell, and in the end she gave up and went upstairs to change.

She looked with some approval in the glass. The strong blue of her suit made her hair look even fairer and fitted her slender figure to perfection. The skirt was pleated, swirling gracefully as she walked, and her burgundy shoes and bag matched each other exactly, the white frilled collar of her blouse accentuating the length of her neck and the delicate shape of her head.

Like me in this, Sky, she prayed, knowing that her prayer would be answered. And then she went down the stairs to meet him.

They were all waiting at the bottom, forming a line for she and Sky to walk past to the door. A sudden suspicion gripped her mind—oh, *please* don't let them have written things all over the car, she begged. But the broad grins and giggles convinced her that they had. Tensely, she held on to Sky's arm, then realised from his own expression that whatever was amusing them all was amusing him too. So it couldn't be graffiti on the car—so what could . . .?

And then they came to the door. The lawn stretched ahead of them, level and flat and sheltered by trees. And a cry of pure delight escaped Sandie's lips.

In the middle of the lawn stood a brand-new wicker basket. Inside it was Con, around it stood Andy and Tim, their hands firmly held on the suede trim. And above it, reaching up into the sky as if impatient to be off, away from the crowds, reared a pure white balloon, rimmed with bands of silver and gold.

'It's your balloon, Sandie,' Sky told her, his arm close about her shoulders. 'Your own balloon—your wedding present. And we're going to start our honeymoon in it—if that's what you want.'

'What I want!' she breathed. 'Oh, *Sky*.'

Together, they climbed into the basket and Con scrambled out, his grin almost splitting his face. Then Sky took over control of the burner, gave the last 'hands off' order and the earth dropped slowly away. Silently, they wafted above the cheering crowd, and for the first time Sandie noticed the streaming coloured banners that hung from the basket like a new form of confetti. She watched as the wedding guests grew smaller and smaller, a freckle of coloured spots on the green lawn. She saw the trees, a Persian carpet of brilliant autumn colour draped across the folded hills. She saw her new home grow tinier and finally disappear as the balloon gained height and drifted further and further away.

Getting married, she thought dreamily, was really very similar to a balloon flight. You started off full of hopes, taking off into the unknown, with very little idea of where you might end up. You couldn't really plan anything—it all depended on which way the wind blew. But, with careful preparation and the right balloon, you could be fairly sure of a good flight and a happy landing.

As she let her fingers twine with his, Sandie knew that her life with Sky was going to be just that. And she turned her face up to her husband's for the first kiss of their honeymoon, knowing that although they might encounter turbulence in their lives together, there would always, always be that happy landing.

 **Harlequin Romance**

## Coming Next Month

**2761 STRANGER IN TOWN Kerry Allyne**
An Australian storekeeper is convinced all gold prospectors are daydreamers, living in a fantasy. Then, falling in love with one of them brings a change of mind—and heart!

**2762 THE DRIFTWOOD DRAGON Ann Charlton**
Haunted by his past, an Australian film star is overjoyed when he finds a woman whose love helps him to shed his typecast image—until his brother's interference almost ruins their chance for happiness.

**2763 VOWS OF THE HEART Susan Fox**
Returning for physical and emotional recovery to the Wyoming ranch where she'd always felt secure, an interior designer discovers her adolescent crush for its owner has turned to love.

**2764 AMARYLLIS DREAMING Samantha Harvey**
Katy finds a man on Amaryllis Island, but not the father she seeks. She finally has to admit, though, that this powerful island overlord is destined to make all her dreams come true.

**2765 ASK ME NO QUESTIONS Valerie Parv**
Trusting her adventurer husband once lead to heartbreak for a Brisbane art-gallery owner. Her return, years later, when she's thinking of marrying someone else, faces her with a once-in-a-lifetime choice.

**2766 TO BRING YOU JOY Essie Summers**
A living legacy gives a young New Zealander the chance to prove her descent from the historic Beauchamps. But her benefactor, dear Aunt Amabel, wants her niece to find adventure—and love.

Available in May wherever paperback books are sold, or through Harlequin Reader Service.

In the U.S.
P.O. Box 1397
Buffalo, N.Y.
14240-1397

In Canada
P.O. Box 2800, Postal Sation A
5170 Yonge Street
Willowdale, Ontario M2N 6J3

# What the press says about Harlequin romance fiction...

"When it comes to romantic novels...
Harlequin is the indisputable king."
— *New York Times*

"...always with an upbeat, happy ending."
— *San Francisco Chronicle*

"Women have come to trust these
stories about contemporary people,
set in exciting foreign places."
— *Best Sellers,* New York

"The most popular reading matter of
American women today."
— *Detroit News*

"...a work of art."
— *Globe & Mail,* Toronto

# What readers say about Harlequin romance fiction...

"I absolutely adore Harlequin romances!
They are fun and relaxing to read, and
each book provides a wonderful escape."
—N.E.,* Pacific Palisades, California

"Harlequin is the best in romantic reading."
—K.G.,* Philadelphia, Pennsylvania

"Harlequins have been my passport to the
world. I have been many places without
ever leaving my doorstep."
—P.Z.,* Belvedere, Illinois

"My praise for the warmth and adventure
your books bring into my life."
—D.F.,*Hicksville, New York

"A pleasant way to relax after a busy day."
—P.W.,* Rector, Arkansas

*Names available on request.

*No one Can Resist . . .*

---

# HARLEQUIN
# REGENCY ROMANCES

---

Regency romances take you back to a time when
men fought for their ladies' honor and passions—a
time when heroines had to choose between love and
duty . . . with love always the winner!

Enjoy these three authentic novels of love and
romance set in one of the most colorful periods of
England's history.

### Lady Alicia's Secret by Rachel Cosgrove Payes

She had to keep her true identity hidden—at least until
she was convinced of his love!

### Deception So Agreeable by Mary Butler

She reacted with outrage to his false proposal of
marriage, then nearly regretted her decision.

### The Country Gentleman by Dinah Dean

She refused to believe the rumors about him—
certainly until they could be confirmed or denied!

---

*Everyone Loves . . .*

# HARLEQUIN GOTHIC ROMANCES

A young woman lured to an isolated estate far from help and civilization . . . a man, lonely, tortured by a centuries' old commitment . . . and a sinister force threatening them both and their newfound love . . . Read these three superb novels of romance and suspense . . . as timeless as love and as filled with the unexpected as tomorrow!

### Return To Shadow Creek by Helen B. Hicks

She returned to the place of her birth—only to discover a sinister plot lurking in wait for her. . . .

### Shadows Over Briarcliff by Marilyn Ross

Her visit vividly brought back the unhappy past—and with it an unknown evil presence. . . .

### The Blue House by Dolores Holliday

She had no control over the evil forces that were driving her to the brink of madness. . . .

# WORLDWIDE LIBRARY IS YOUR TICKET TO ROMANCE, ADVENTURE AND EXCITEMENT

## Experience it all in these big, bold Bestsellers— Yours exclusively from WORLDWIDE LIBRARY WHILE QUANTITIES LAST

To receive these Bestsellers, complete the order form, detach and send together with your check or money order (include 75¢ postage and handling), payable to WORLDWIDE LIBRARY, to:

**In the U.S.**
WORLDWIDE LIBRARY
901 Fuhrmann Blvd.
Buffalo, N.Y. 14269

**In Canada**
WORLDWIDE LIBRARY
P.O. Box 2800, 5170 Yonge Street
Postal Station A, Willowdale, Ontario
M2N 6J3

| Quant. | Title | Price |
|---|---|---|
| | WILD CONCERTO, Anne Mather | $2.95 |
| | A VIOLATION, Charlotte Lamb | $3.50 |
| | SECRETS, Sheila Holland | $3.50 |
| | SWEET MEMORIES, LaVyrle Spencer | $3.50 |
| | FLORA, Anne Weale | $3.50 |
| | SUMMER'S AWAKENING, Anne Weale | $3.50 |
| | FINGER PRINTS, Barbara Delinsky | $3.50 |
| | DREAMWEAVER, Felicia Gallant/Rebecca Flanders | $3.50 |
| | EYE OF THE STORM, Maura Seger | $3.50 |
| | HIDDEN IN THE FLAME, Anne Mather | $3.50 |
| | ECHO OF THUNDER, Maura Seger | $3.95 |
| | DREAM OF DARKNESS, Jocelyn Haley | $3.95 |
| | | |
| | YOUR ORDER TOTAL | $_____ |
| | New York and Arizona residents add appropriate sales tax | $_____ |
| | Postage and Handling | $__.75 |
| | I enclose | $_____ |

NAME _____

ADDRESS _____ APT.# _____

CITY _____

STATE/PROV. _____ ZIP/POSTAL CODE _____

WW-1-3